A I HE
HIGHLANDS

Barbara Cartland

Barbara Cartland Ebooks Ltd

ISBNs

978-1-78867-815-5 EPUB

978-1-78867-816-2 PAPERBACK

Book design by M-Y Books
m-ybooks.co.uk

AUDIOBOOKS

Listen to all your favourite Barbara Cartland Audio Books for free on Spotify, just point your phone camera at this code or go to **https://rb.gy/tx6vrl**

THE BARBARA CARTLAND ETERNAL COLLECTION

The Barbara Cartland Eternal Collection is the unique opportunity to collect all five hundred of the timeless beautiful romantic novels written by the world's most celebrated and enduring romantic author.

Named the Eternal Collection because Barbara's inspiring stories of pure love, just the same as love itself, the books will be published on the internet at the rate of four titles per month until all five hundred are available.

The Eternal Collection, classic pure romance available worldwide for all time .

THE LATE DAME BARBARA CARTLAND

Barbara Cartland, who sadly died in May 2000 at the grand age of nincty eight, remains one of the world's most famous romantic novelists. With worldwide sales of over one billion, her outstanding 723 books have been translated into thirty six different languages, to be enjoyed by readers of romance globally.

Writing her first book 'Jigsaw' at the age of 21, Barbara bccamc an immediate bestseller. Building upon this initial success, she wrote continuously throughout her life, producing bestsellers for an astonishing 76 years. In addition to Barbara Cartland's legion of fans in the UK and across Europe, her books have always been immensely popular in the USA. In 1976 she achieved the unprecedented feat of having books at numbers 1 & 2 in the prestigious B. Dalton Bookseller bestsellers list.

Although she is often referred to as the 'Queen of Romance', Barbara Cartland also wrote several historical biographies, six autobiographies and numerous theatrical plays as well as books on life, love, health and cookery. Becoming one of Britain's most popular media personalities and dressed in her trademark pink, Barbara spoke on radio and television about social and political issues, as well as making many public appearances.

In 1991 she became a Dame of the Order of the British Empire for her contribution to literature and her work for humanitarian and charitable causes.

Known for her glamour, style, and vitality Barbara Cartland became a legend in her own lifetime. Best remembered for her wonderful romantic novels and loved by millions of readers worldwide, her books remain treasured for their heroic heroes, plucky heroines and traditional values. But above all, it was Barbara Cartland's overriding belief in the positive power of love to help, heal and improve the quality of life for everyone that made her truly unique.

AUTHOR'S NOTE

"My heart's in the Highlands, my heart is not here,
My heart's in the Highlands a-chasing the deer.
Chasing the wild deer, and following the roe,
My heart's in the Highlands, wherever I go."

This verse, written by Robert Burns, is true of every Scot.

It is difficult to explain how the spirit of Scotland is so much a part of one's breathing and feeling that the moment one crosses the border, one is vitally aware of it. I am extremely proud that my grandmother – my father's mother – was a Falkner and a descendant of Robert the Bruce.

My great-grandmother was a descendant of the Dukes of Hamilton. My mother was a Scobell, one of the oldest Saxon families in existence, who were living in Devonshire long before the Norman Conquest in 1066. Yet she had both my brothers and me all christened with "Hamilton" as one of our names.

My married name was McCorquodale, and when I caught my first salmon in the Helmsdale River in 1928, it was one of the most exciting experiences of my life.

The story is really set in Sutherland, and the castle I describe is the magnificent home of the Dukes of Sutherland.

Marriage by Consent was legal in Scotland until 1949.

Yseulta is Celtic and is pronounced "Eezulta".

CHAPTER ONE
1885

The Duke of Strathvegon thought with a sigh of relief that the state dinner was coming to an end. He felt the quality of the food had not done justice to the beauty of the dining room, which owed its proportions and its pictures to George IV.

Whenever possible, he avoided the invitations that he received so frequently from the Prince of Wales. Princess Alexandra, looking ravishingly lovely as usual, rose to her feet and the ladies processed with a fluttering of gowns and a glitter of jewels towards the door.

As they did so the Duke looked at the Countess of Wallington and thought she was looking unusually pale. She was, without exception, the most beautiful woman in London. The diamonds and sapphires of her necklace showed off the translucent whiteness of her skin, and her blue eyes shone like stars.

As she passed him there was an expression in them that he did not understand, but he knew perceptively that something was wrong. He wondered what it could possibly be, and as the Prince of Wales beckoned to him to come to the top of the table and sit next to him, he found it difficult to concentrate on what His Royal Highness was saying.

The Duke was in fact thinking of how passionate Hermione Wallington had been last night.

He had thought as he walked home at dawn that he had seldom been involved in a more satisfactory *affaire de coeur*. Now as the Prince of Wales began to talk about horses and the rest of the male guests joined in, the Duke for the moment forgot the Countess. In fact he made several witty remarks, which caused His Royal Highness to laugh uproariously.

When they joined the ladies, already some of the guests wore the restless look of those who wished the evening would come to a close.

As soon as the Prince and Princess of Wales had said goodnight to their Guest of Honour and processed from the room, there was a general chorus of goodbyes among everybody who remained.

Hermione Wallington, as one of Princess Alexandra's ladies-in-waiting, was expected to follow almost immediately in the wake of the royal couple. She therefore curtsied to the Guest of Honour with a grace that the Duke appreciated, then held out her hand to him. As she did so he felt something pressed against his palm, and he quickly closed his fingers over it.

"Goodnight, Your Grace," Hermione murmured formally.

Then after bidding several other goodnights, she moved towards the door. It was impossible for the Duke to see what she had handed to him until some of the other guests had said their farewells and moved away. Only by walking to one of the windows, as if anxious to see if it was raining or fine, was he able to look surreptitiously at what he had transferred to his left hand.

On a tiny slip of paper was written in very small handwriting,

'Come to me at once – I am desperate!'

For a moment the Duke stared as if he could not believe his eyes. Then a deep voice beside him said,

"Are you worrying, My Lord Duke, in case it is raining and the ground is too soft for your horse tomorrow?"

With an effort the Duke remembered that he had a horse running at Epsom, and he replied,

"Actually, Prime Minister, I was thinking of how unpleasant it will be if I have to watch him in the pouring rain!"

The Prime Minister smiled.

"I sympathise with you, but I think in fact the weather will be fine."

At any other time the Duke would have waited to talk to Mr. Gladstone. He was sorry for him because the Queen could not hide her dislike and mistrust of him. She blamed him for the death of General Gordon at Khartoum at the beginning of the year. In the music halls he was referred to as 'M.O.G.' – Murderer of Gordon.

The Duke always went out of his way to be pleasant to a man when he was "down", and he was sure that as Prime Minister Mr. Gladstone's days were numbered. But for the moment Hermione's cry for help was all that mattered.

The servants in their powdered wigs called his, carriage and when he stepped into it, he looked again at the piece of paper. He found Hermione's words hard to decipher in the flickering light of the candle-lanterns. But having re-read the message he wondered what could possibly have occurred. Last night they had agreed that they would not meet tonight but would dine together the following evening. The Earl of Wallington was not due back from Paris, where he had been sent on a special mission by the Prime Minister, until the following day.

"I shall be counting the hours until we can be together again," Hermione had said in her soft seductive voice. "At the same time, it will be too obvious if we leave Buckingham Palace at the same time and neither of us is seen elsewhere that evening."

"I agree with you," the Duke answered, "And I will go to White's. There will certainly be a number of gossip-mongers in the club who will be aware of my presence."

Hermione moved a little closer to him before she said,

"I will look in at the party that is taking place at Devonshire House."

She sighed before she added,

"It will be agony when we might be together, but we have to be careful because George is very jealous."

The Duke had kissed her and thought as he did so that it was not surprising the Earl was jealous of anything so lovely Hermione Wallington had stunned London from the moment she had appeared on the social scene at the age of seventeen-and-a-half. It was impossible for the raffish members of the clubs in St. James's Street not to go into eulogies over her beauty.

It was inevitable she should have made a brilliant marriage in her first Season. The betting had been at first on a somewhat elderly Marquess who was looking for a second wife to give him the heir he had not managed to produce with his first. Then the Earl of Wallington, rich, distinguished, and only twenty years older than Hermione, had swept her off her feet.

He married her, to the extreme satisfaction of her parents a month before the Season ended.

She had dutifully and rapidly produced a son and a daughter. Then she had emerged from the country. She had struck the social scene in London once again like a meteor from outer space.

By this time the Earl had an important post in the Ministry of Foreign Affairs which meant he was often absent on diplomatic missions abroad, for which it was impossible for his wife always to accompany him. She had no wish to miss the adulation of the men who flocked to her husband's house in Berkeley Square.

When she took her first lover, Hermione was so terrified of being discovered that it was therefore not a very enjoyable episode. The next two were pleasant interludes, but when she met the Duke she fell in love.

It was not surprising. He stood out amongst the tall, distinguished aristocrats who filled the Drawing Rooms of the most brilliant and exclusive society in Europe. Being Scottish made the Duke seem different from other men. He had inherited not only his fair hair from a Viking ancestor who had invaded Scottish shores, but also his height and strong physique.

When he wore Highland dress, he was so devastatingly fascinating that no woman was too old to find her heart beating faster when she looked at him.

For the first time in her life Hermione lost her heart completely. She had been delighted to become a Countess before her eighteenth birthday and was fond of her husband, although she was frightened of him.

She had however, no idea of the delights and sensual joys of passion until she met the Duke. In fact he had awakened her to a womanhood she had never known before. She gave him not only her body and her heart but also what she believed was her soul.

Hermione was not particularly intelligent and as was then usual in aristocratic families had been inadequately educated by an inexperienced Governess. A middle-aged woman, she knew little herself, and what she did know she had no idea how to impart to her pupils.

Hermione's brothers had been sent to Eton, then Oxford, while she read a few dull history books and fumbled over the multiplication tables. She found her lessons boring, especially those that involved writing out long extracts from what her Governess considered to be the classics.

The Duke, however, was not concerned with Hermione's brain. Her body was entrancing, and he had only to look at her beauty to realise she had a charm that was the envy of every other woman in the room. He was too experienced not to realise that her love for him had changed her from being, despite her marriage, little more than an unopened bud into a rose in full bloom.

Because he was aware of how indiscreet and impulsive women could be, he had admonished her very seriously to be careful where her husband was concerned.

"You must show him a lot of affection," he had said sternly, "And, for goodness' sake, listen to what he is saying to you."

"It is difficult, when I am thinking of you," Hermione had replied.

"I know," the Duke replied. "At the same time, if he suspects, he may prevent us from seeing each other."

She had given a cry of horror and flung her arms around him.

"I cannot lose you, Kenyon! How can I? I love you, *I love you!* If I were not allowed to see you again … I should *die!*"

She spoke wildly and the Duke knew it was dangerous.

"Now listen, my beautiful one," he said, "You have to be sensible and, promise me, as you have done before, that you will not confide in anyone."

He knew as he spoke how difficult it could be for a woman in love not to talk about it to her closest friend.

The inevitable result was that the story was carried all over London within twenty-four hours.

"I have kept my promise," Hermione assured him. "I have not told anyone, and the only person who is aware that I see you is my lady's maid."

The Duke knew that in any love affair there always had to be what the French called a *complice d'amour*. He had been assured over and over again, however, that Jones adored her mistress and would never betray her.

His carriage turned off the Mall, passed St. James's Palace, and proceeded up St. James's Street, as he wondered anxiously what could have gone wrong. As he passed White's Club he thought it was a mistake that he was not going in, as they had planned.

He had told one of his friends earlier in the day that he would play cards with him as soon as he could get away from the Palace. The carriage drew up outside Wallington House in Berkeley Square. As the Duke stepped out he said to his footman,

"I will walk home."

He did not raise his hand to the silver knocker but, as he expected, the door opened. As he went inside he saw there was only Jones, the lady's maid, in the hall. The night-footman had been sent to bed and, as he had last night, the Duke moved towards the staircase.

"Her Ladyship's in the Morning Room, Your Grace," Jones said in a whisper.

The Duke raised his eyebrows, but he did not ask any questions. He merely walked from the staircase across the hall and into the Morning Room at the far end. It was an attractive room with windows looking on to a small garden at the back of the house, but Hermione had never waited for him there before. Always she had been in her *boudoir* when he arrived, wearing a diaphanous *negligée* that revealed rather than concealed her attractions.

Now as he entered the room he saw that she had not changed from the elaborate gown she had been wearing at Buckingham Palace, although she had removed her sapphire tiara. She gave a muffled cry as he entered and jumped up from the sofa on which she had been sitting.

The Duke shut the door and walked towards her.

"What has happened?" he asked.

The words had barely passed his lips before Hermione had flung herself against him, holding on to him convulsively and hiding her face against his shoulder.

His arms went round her and he asked again,

"What has upset you? What is wrong?"

"Oh, Kenyon … Kenyon, how can I tell you?" Hermione sobbed.

He could feel her body trembling against him.

He held her close, his lips on her hair, which smelt of an exotic French perfume.

"H-how, how can I bear it? Oh, Kenyon what am I to do?"

The Duke moved her gently towards the sofa.

He sat down and pulled her close against him saying as he did so."

"Now stop crying, my sweet, and tell me exactly what has happened. Then we will decide what to do."

"I-I was so frightened you would not come tonight."

"But I am here!" he said. "So tell me what I have to hear."

Hermione raised her head, and now in the candlelight he could see the tears running down her cheeks. He thought she looked even lovelier than she had at Buckingham Palace earlier in the evening.

"George has ... found out!" she stammered.

It was what the Duke had expected. At the same time, it was a shock to hear her say so.

"How does he know?" he asked. "Has he returned?"

"N-no. He has not yet returned. But when he does he is going to k-kill you!"

The Duke stared at her for a moment before he remarked,

"I think that is unlikely."

"He is, *he is!*" Hermione insisted. "He is going to challenge you to a duel. And he is determined that you shall die."

"I am sure you are exaggerating," the Duke said dryly. "At the same time, how do you know this?"

As he spoke he took the handkerchief from his breast-pocket and gently wiped the tears from Hermione's cheeks.

"What are we to do? How can we face it?" she asked.

"First of all answer my question," the Duke said quietly. "How do you know that your husband is aware of what is happening?"

Hermione gave a little choked sob.

"George's valet Dawkins is courting Jones. He wrote to her from Paris saying that George has had us watched for some time and that a report had come to him with some papers from the Foreign Office, which were carried by Courier because they were urgent."

The Duke's lips tightened before he asked,

"You had someone following you, and you had no idea of it?"

"How could I have known? How could I have guessed?" Hermione asked. "Oh, Kenyon, how can I let you die. How can I live without you?"

As she finished speaking, she flung her arms round the Duke's neck and pulled his head down to hers. He kissed her, but his mind was concerned with what she had just told him. As he raised his head again he said,

"Tell me exactly what the valet said."

"He said," Hermione replied in a choked voice, "That George was furious and swore he would kill you! He will challenge you to a duel immediately on his return!"

"When is he coming back?" the Duke asked.

He knew as he did so that he was in a very compromising position.

"Not until Friday," Hermione replied. "He has an important meeting tomorrow and there is a dinner that I am sure he cannot refuse to attend."

The Duke thought that would give them a little time.

Then, as he did not speak, Hermione cried,

"Think of the scandal! Think how furious the Queen will be when she has forbidden duelling."

"But it still takes place," the Duke remarked.

"If George kills you, I shall have to go abroad with him for at least three or four years. Oh, Kenyon ... how could I bear that? How could I give up everything?"

Without thinking she glanced down at the miniature on her shoulder, which was worn by all the ladies-in-waiting to Princess Alexandra. The Duke rose from the sofa to walk to the fireplace and stand with his back to the flower-filled hearth.

"We have to be clever about this Hermione," he said.

"How do you mean clever?" she asked. "George will come back and challenge you to a duel – and how can you refuse without being branded a coward?"

The Duke did not answer and she went on,

"I shall be accused of causing your death and no one will ever speak to me again."

She burst into tears and there was nothing the Duke could do but go back to the sofa and put his arms around her. She wept against him, and he held her close for a little while before he said,

"Now listen, my dearest, what is important is that you must deny everything of which you are accused."

"But George will not believe me!" Hermione sobbed. "You know how jealous he is. He has threatened before to leave one of his relatives in the house with me when he goes away."

She sobbed again before she went on,

"What that means is that he would have somebody spying on me and telling him everything I do, everybody I meet."

The Duke thought that perhaps a relative might have been easier to deal with than an unknown spy, but there seemed to be no point in saying so now. It seemed incredible that he had been so stupid as not to expect the jealous Earl might have had his wife watched.

As he thought about it, he remembered that George Wallington was known for his quick temper. He was also, in the words of some of his friends, "Unpredictably fiery when the occasion demanded it."

He had the idea that when the Earl thought it over he would not kill him, as he had threatened to do, but he could quite easily wound him severely. Apart from the physical aspect of it, the scandal would undoubtedly reverberate throughout the whole of Mayfair.

It was inevitable that being so beautiful Hermione had made a great number of women envious. They would be only too delighted to have the chance of tipping her off the pedestal on which she had been placed.

This was not only because of her husband's importance, but also as lady-in-waiting to Princess Alexandra.

The Duke, when he chose to use it, had a very quick brain. Now he was thinking intently of some way by which he could avoid what he was aware would be a catastrophe both for himself and for Hermione. He drew her a little closer to him. Then he said,

"Now listen, my sweet, it is very important that you should do exactly what I tell you."

"How can I listen when all I want to do is cry?" Hermione asked.

"That is something you must not do," the Duke replied.

"H-how can I help it?"

"You have to help it," the Duke insisted, "Because you have to act your part very convincingly."

"What part?"

She looked up at him pathetically, and he thought that although she was twenty-five she looked both young and helpless. There was a tender expression in his eyes as he said,

"We are in a mess, but somehow we are going to get out of it."

"How ... how?" she asked.

"First you must pretend you know nothing of these accusations – do you understand? – *nothing!* When your husband comes back you must appear to be astounded and completely bewildered that he should think anything so unkind and so cruel when he knows you love him."

"But I do not love him!" Hermione whispered. "I love *you!*"

Once again the tears filled her eyes and began to run down her cheeks.

"As I love you!" the Duke replied. "At the same time, I shall not be much use to you if I am dead, and you do not want to give up the parties and balls and be buried in the country where you will see no one."

Hermione was listening.

Then as he finished speaking she gave a little cry.

"I forgot – I forgot to tell you. I shall not be buried in the country! George is going to divorce me!"

The Duke stiffened.

"Is that what he said?"

"Dawkins put it at the very end of the letter and I did not dare tell you. But if you are ... dead and am divorced – there will be no one to marry me!"

The Duke suddenly felt that he had stepped into a maze and could find no way out. Then he told himself that if Hermione was panicking he must keep his head. Once again she had hidden her face against his shoulder and was crying convulsively.

He held her close while his brain was racing round and round trying to find a way out of the prison walls which seemed to be closing in upon him. Once again he managed to say quietly,

"We have to save ourselves, and you must, and I repeat *must,* Hermione, do exactly what I am telling you to do."

She raised her head.

"I-I will try."

"That is what I want you to say," he said, "And I want you, too, to be very brave."

He repeated slowly as if to a small child exactly what he had already said. She must pretend complete innocence, and above all must look happy and untroubled. She must not for a moment let anyone suspect that she was at all worried about anything.

"H-how can I do that," Hermione asked, "When I shall be waiting in terror for George's return?"

"You have to act the part," the Duke said quietly, "As cleverly as if you were on the stage at Drury Lane with an audience watching you."

He went over it once again. Then he said,

"Tomorrow morning I shall go riding in the park, and if we meet, by chance, I shall be able to tell you what else I have planned."

"Riding in the Park?" Hermione repeated he thought rather stupidly. "But why should we do that?"

"Then people who see you will not suspect that you are upset about anything, but we are only delighted to meet each other."

"I-I do not understand."

"The worst thing you could possibly do would be to sit in the house weeping," the Duke said. "If we are being watched, perhaps by somebody in your household, then it will be reported to your husband who will undoubtedly take it as further evidence of your infidelity."

Hermione gave a cry of sheer horror, and the Duke went on,

"In the meantime, I am sure I can think of some way by which I can prevent myself from becoming involved in a duel."

"How can you do that?" Hermione enquired helplessly.

"I could go abroad, for one thing," the Duke suggested.

"Then everybody will know – and be quite certain of our guilt," Hermione said, "Especially as you have horses running at all the race meetings!"

The Duke thought that was the first intelligent comment she had made so far, but he merely replied,

"I am sure there is a way out of this and all I need is time to think of it. Now, please, my dearest, do exactly what I have asked of you – act brilliantly the part of a very beautiful and happy young wife."

"But I am not happy, only desperately miserable!" Hermione protested.

The Duke decided that words were superfluous. He kissed Hermione and caressed her until her tears were forgotten, at least for the moment. Then, as if he realised it was growing late, he rose to his feet.

"I am going to leave you now," he said, "But we will meet in the park tomorrow morning, apparently talking cheerfully about tonight's dinner party at Buckingham Palace, and nothing more serious."

"Oh, Kenyon. I am sure I shall break down and cry!" Hermione said.

"If you do, you will spoil everything," the Duke said. "Now trust me and, if you love me, do exactly what I have told you to do."

He kissed her again to prevent her from saying any more. As she realised he was really going she held out her arms.

"Kenyon please ... stay with me," she pleaded.

"Not tonight," the Duke said, "And I think, apart from the danger, it would be an anti-climax because of the way you are feeling at the moment."

"Whatever I am feeling, *I love you!*"

He kissed her again, then as she still tried to cling on to him he walked to the door.

"Ten o'clock tomorrow morning in the Row," he said, "And look your most beautiful, which is how I want to see you."

He opened the door before she could stop him and going into the hall shut it behind him. Jones was sitting in the padded chair normally occupied by the night-footman. The Duke pressed several gold sovereigns into her palm and as she opened the front door said,

"Take care of your mistress and thank you for warning us."

"Look after y'rself, Your Grace," Jones replied. "The Master's got a nasty temper when he's roused!"

The Duke did not reply.

He hurried out of the house, hoping the watcher was not still on duty. He walked quickly down Hill Street and from South Street into Park Lane. Strathvegon House was a large and important mansion, which had been built by his grandfather fifty years earlier.

The pictures that covered the walls had been in the family for generations but did not compare at all favourably with those in the Royal Collection. The Duke, however, was very conscious of his ancestors as he walked into the large, impressive hall. He handed his hat and cape to the footman on duty, and without speaking walked up the stairs.

As he did so he felt a strong desire to talk to his mother. She was staying with him, having come down from Scotland where she lived most of the year. She wanted to be present at several Court functions which took place at that time of year, and which she particularly enjoyed.

It was nearly midnight, but the Duke was sure his mother would still be awake and reading, as she habitually did until the early hours of the morning. He therefore walked towards the bedroom she occupied and which had been hers ever since she had married.

He knocked on the door and heard his mother's voice say,

"Come in!"

The Duchess was sitting up against her pillows looking, despite her age, extremely attractive. She had been a great beauty when she was young. But she differed from Hermione Wallington in being not only beautiful but also extremely intelligent. Having three brothers older than herself she had shared their Tutors.

She had found the acquisition of knowledge fascinating. Her brothers, however, had teased her and predicted that if she continued to be so clever she would frighten away all her prospective suitors and remain an old maid for the rest of her life.

Her beauty however had prevented that from happening – she married the Duke of Strathvegon a month after her eighteenth birthday. It had been a very happy marriage, the only sadness being that, having produced a son and heir, the Duchess was unable to have any more children.

It was inevitable therefore that she should spoil her only child. As she looked up now, there was an expression of admiration on her face as her son came towards her.

"You are back early!" she exclaimed in surprise.

The Duke did not answer but stooped to kiss her cheek before he sat down on the side of her bed.

Then as she put out her hand towards him, he took it in both of his and said,

"Mama, I am in trouble!"

"In trouble?" the Duchess exclaimed., "What has happened?"

The Duke did not answer, and after a moment the Duchess added,

"I suppose it concerns Hermione Wallington!"

"Why should you say that?" the Duke asked.

"Because, my darling, you have been making rather an exhibition of yourself, and of course everybody is talking. How could they do anything else?"

"I was under the illusion that we had been comparatively discreet!" the Duke answered.

The Duchess gave a little shrug of her shoulders.

"You know as well as I do that gossip is carried on the wind, and it comes not only from clubs and *boudoirs,* but also from servants' halls!"

"By that I suppose you mean your lady's maid told you!"

He knew that his mother heard quite a lot from old Janet, who had been with her since she was a girl and who really should have been retired years ago.

"Never mind how I heard it," the Duchess said. "Tell me how you are in trouble."

The Duke drew in his breath.

"George Wallington has had us watched and is threatening to kill me in a duel and divorce Hermione!"

The Duchess stifled a cry but her fingers tightened on his.

Then she said,

"That is something which must be prevented, and quickly! When does he return from Paris?"

"On Friday," the Duke replied.

He thought as he spoke that it was so like his mother that she should ask the important questions first instead of exclaiming in horror at the situation.

"Friday," the Duchess mused, "And he will arrive in the afternoon?"

"I suppose so," the Duke agreed.

"Then we can leave for Scotland in your private train just before luncheon."

The Duke stared at her.

"Leave for Scotland? Why should we do that?"

"Because, my dearest Kenyon, when we reach the castle you are going to choose the girl you wish to marry and will immediately announce your engagement!"

The Duke stared at his mother as if she had taken leave of her senses.

"What are you saying? I do not understand!"

The Duchess sighed.

"Darling, I have been begging you for years to get married and have a son. After all, you owe it to the family, and more especially to the clan!"

"Mother, I have heard all that before!" the Duke said sharply. "But, surely..."

"Do not be foolish," the Duchess interrupted. "First of all, if we are in Scotland, George Wallington cannot challenge you to a duel. Secondly, if you announce your engagement, he can hardly at the same time declare that you are his wife's lover and sue for a divorce!"

She saw that her son was still staring at her in sheer astonishment as she went on,

"Divorce proceedings through the House of Lords are always long-drawn-out, and take months, if not years, to set in motion."

"I know, I know," the Duke said, "But…"

"There are no 'buts'," the Duchess interrupted. "George Wallington will not make a fool of himself by dragging up a man's past at the very moment he is being married with the congratulations and good wishes of his friends."

There was silence until the Duke said,

"I understand what you are suggesting, Mama, but you have forgotten that it is impossible to be married unless one has a bride!"

"I have thought of that," the Duchess replied. "I have recently noticed three girls, any of whom I am sure would make you a good wife and would grace the position they would hold as your Duchess."

"You are bewildering me!" the Duke protested.

"I know it is rather a shock," his mother said. "At the same time, there is nothing else you can do in the circumstances."

"I shall be running away," the Duke objected.

"On the contrary," his mother replied, "You will be retiring until you can reinforce your position!"

There was a twinkle in the eyes of the Duchess as she spoke and the Duke, as if he could not help himself, laughed.

Then he said,

"All right, Mama, you win! You have been nagging me for years to get married, and I might have guessed you would not miss the opportunity when it occurred."

"You must see, dearest, that it is the only possible solution, although I would rather you could marry somebody you loved."

There was a wistful note in the Duchess's voice, which her son did not miss, but he said harshly,

"If I cannot marry the woman I do love, what does it matter? Choose anyone you like, and if she pleases the clan, that should be sufficient!"

As if he could not bear to say any more, he walked out of the room, closing the door quietly behind him. The Duchess sat very still, looking after him. Then as tears came into her eyes, she said softly beneath her breath,

"My poor darling, but there really is no other way."

CHAPTER TWO

The Duke of Charnwood looked up from the letter he was reading, at his wife who was sitting on the opposite side of the breakfast table.

"This note is from Elizabeth Strathvegon," he said. "It was delivered by a groom and was marked *'URGENT'!"*

"What does it say?" the Duchess asked vaguely.

She was thinking as she spoke that her daughter Beryl had been a huge success at Devonshire House last night. But she would certainly be in need of several more gowns if she was to accept all the invitations she had received. The Duke was silent as he read the letter. Then he gave an exclamation.

"Now I know the reason for this," he said. "Wallington has found out, and Strathvegon is running for cover!"

"What are you talking about?" the Duchess demanded.

The Duke read a few more lines of the letter before he replied,

"Elizabeth Strathvegon is inviting Beryl to stay in Scotland for a ball she intends to givc at the beginning of next week."

"Scotland!" the Duchess exclaimed. "In the middle of the Season? I have never heard of such a thing!"

"Do not be foolish," the Duke replied. "Young Strathvegon has gone too far for once, and Elizabeth is making sure that she can announce his engagement at the ball."

His wife stared at him in astonishment before she said,

"I still do not know what you are talking about. If that spoilt young man has ever been in love with anyone except himself, he is in love with Hermione Wallington, who in my opinion is behaving abominably while her husband is in Paris."

"Everybody knows that," the Duke replied, "but if you want to see Beryl wearing strawberry leaves on her head, then she had better pack her bags and be on the private train, which Elizabeth Strathvegon says..."

He paused to look down at the letter and continued,

"…is leaving King's Cross at twelve noon tomorrow morning."

There was a sudden cry from Lady Beryl Wood, who was sitting beside her father. She had been paying little attention to what he was saying as she ate her eggs and bacon. Now she stared at the Duke with a frightened expression in her eyes as she said,

"Are you saying, Papa, that the Duke of Strathvegon intends to propose to me?"

"It is perfectly clear to me," the Duke replied. "The Duchess has got the wind up, and I would not mind betting a thousand pounds to a threepenny bit that Strathvegon's engagement will be in the '*Gazette*' next week."

"But not to me!" Lady Beryl exclaimed.

"Why not?" the Duke asked. "Strathvegon may have 'sowed his wild oats' rather more enthusiastically than was necessary, but he own thousands of acres in Scotland, and his racehorses have won several prizes already this year."

Lady Beryl gave another horrified cry and now it was shriller than it had been before.

"But, Papa, you promised that if Roland could make a success with his cattle and his blood-mares we could become engaged in the Autumn."

"I said I would *consider* it," the Duke amended loftily, "but Strathvegon is a different proposition from an impoverished young Baronet."

"That is unfair," Lady Beryl said heatedly. "Roland is not impoverished. He is merely handicapped at the moment by the death duties on his father's estate, and you have said often enough that his family is one of the oldest in England. No one can say he is not 'Blue-blooded'!"

"Nevertheless," the Duke said firmly, "he is not to be compared with Strathvegon."

"But, Papa, I love him. I love Roland, and I have no wish to marry the Duke, or anyone else."

"You will marry whom I choose," the Duke argued, "and if Strathvegon asks you, which he appears to be about to do, you will accept him!"

Lady Beryl threw her knife and fork down on the plate.

"I will marry no one but Roland!" she flashed. "It is cruel, very cruel of you, Papa, to go back on your word."

As she spoke she burst into tears and ran from the room, slamming the door behind her.

The Duchess looked after her daughter in consternation.

Then she said,

"Really, William, I see no point in upsetting Beryl in this way. Considering the way the Duke has been behaving with Hermione Wallington, I cannot believe he is thinking of marrying anyone."

The Duke often found his wife rather stupid, and he knew he would have to explain exactly what was occurring in words of two syllables. At the same time, he told himself, that Strathvegon was a matrimonial catch that should not be missed. Although he liked the young man with whom his daughter had fallen in love, he had, because she was so beautiful, been disappointed that she had not, in his own words, ‘Hooked a bigger fish’.

As the Duchess of Strathvegon, she would certainly shine amongst the peeresses at the Opening of Parliament. When she married she would also become, and sooner than he had expected, a Lady of the Bedchamber to the Queen.

Aloud he said,

“I am going to explain to you, my dear, why all this is happening. Then you will have to hurry and see that Beryl’s clothes are packed so that she can travel North with the Duchess in the Duke’s private train tomorrow.”

“But, William...” the Duchess began to expostulate.

She knew however by the expression on her husband’s face that he was not going to listen to her.

*

At almost the same time, the Earl of Fernhurst was opening a note from the Duchess of Strathvegon, which had been delivered at his house by a groom on horseback. It was waiting for him on the breakfast table on top of a pile of envelopes, which he suspected contained bills. The mere thought of his overdraft at the bank made his temper rise.

He however was curious enough to open the Duchess's letter before he looked at the others and gave an exclamation of delight.

"What do you think of this, Mary?" he asked his wife.

She was pouring out the coffee for her two daughters, Deborah who was eighteen and a debutante, and Maisie, who was two years younger.

"Think of what?" Mary answered vaguely.

"The Duchess of Strathvegon has invited Deborah to stay with her at Strathvegon Castle. She is to join the Duke's private train at King's Cross on Friday morning at noon!"

Deborah, who was fair-haired with blue eyes, gave a cry of excitement.

"Oh, Papa, a private train! I have never been in one!"

"Well, you are going in one now," her father said, "and if you play your cards cleverly, you will own it!"

Deborah laughed as if her father had said something funny.

"Are you suggesting, Papa, that the Duke will give it to me as a present?"

"With all his other worldly goods, if he marries you," the Earl replied.

"*Marries* me?" Deborah gasped. "Are you joking, Papa?"

"What are you talking about, Henry?" the Countess enquired. "I can assure you that Kenyon Strathvegon is not looking in Deborah's direction at the moment."

She gave a meaningful glance at her husband and he replied,

"I am well aware of that, but if Wallington has turned nasty, as everybody is expecting him to do, then Strathvegon, unless he wants to cause the biggest scandal since Melbourne was cited as a co-respondent, has to do something about it."

"Are you suggesting," the Countess, who was quick-witted, asked, "that he intends to be married?"

"If you ask me, it is the only possible way he can escape, and George Wallington in a temper is not someone I would like to meet on a dark night!"

The Countess stared at her husband.

"I suppose you know what you are talking about," she asked, "but when I was having tea with Amy yesterday, she said..."

She stopped, looked at her two daughters, and said quickly,

"... I will tell you afterwards."

The Earl was once again reading the Duchess's letter.

"Well, I always hoped," he said, "that Deborah would make a good match with somebody who was 'warm in the pocket', but I never aspired as high as Strathvegon!"

"The Duke is very handsome, Papa," Deborah said, "but he has never asked me to dance with him."

"You are being asked to the castle to dance with him now," the Earl said, "and if you miss this chance, let me make it quite clear, that we shall have to go to the country and stay there!"

Deborah gave a little cry of protest.

"But the Season has only just started," the Countess objected.

"I know that," the Earl replied, "but these *damned* bills have to be paid somehow, and who better to do it than Strathvegon?"

"I think the Duke is very handsome!" Deborah giggled.

"So do I!" her sister Maisie joined in. "I have watched him riding in the park, and he rides much better than any other man!"

"That reminds me," the Countess said. "I think one of the carriage horses is lame."

The Earl rose from the table holding the Duchess's letter in his hand.

"The groom is waiting for an answer," he said "and I am going to tell the Duchess that Deborah will be at the station at twelve noon, as invited. If she comes back engaged to the Duke, you can have new carriage horses. If not, I must sell the lot!"

He walked from the breakfast room as he spoke and the Countess looked at her eldest daughter with satisfaction.

"Now, dearest," she said, "we have to decide what you are to wear in Scotland, as it will certainly be cooler than it is here."

*

The Marquess of Derroncorde came in to breakfast wearing his riding clothes, since when he was in London he invariably rode before breakfast. One of the girls seated at the breakfast table rose when he entered and hurried to the dishes that were laid out on the sideboard. There were no servants in attendance at breakfast time, though at other meals the Marquess, who enjoyed pomp and circumstance, was waited on by a butler and two footmen.

"Will you have eggs this morning, Uncle Lionel," Yseulta enquired, "or haddock?"

Although she spoke with a soft, musical note in her voice, there was an expression of nervousness in her eyes, which was invariably there when she spoke to her uncle.

"Haddock!" the Marquess replied sharply.

He sat down at the breakfast table, and as he did so his wife poured out a cup of coffee. She passed it to his daughter Sarah to put down beside him.

"There is a letter for you, Lionel," the Countess said, "which arrived about a quarter-of-an-hour ago. The groom, I understand, is waiting for a reply."

"Who is it from?" the Marquess enquired.

"I have of course not opened it," his wife replied, "but Johnson thought the groom was wearing the Strathvegon livery."

"Strathvegon?" the Marquess exclaimed. "What does that young popinjay want of me?"

The Marchioness sighed.

"Now, Lionel," she said, "do not be vindictive just because his horse beat yours last week at Newmarket. After all, it was a close finish, and I thought in fact that His Grace had the better jockey."

"I disagree with you!" the Marquess said angrily. "I would not have run Red Rufus in that race had I known that Strathvegon was running Crusader. He entered at the last minute, and if you ask me it was a dirty trick that should be brought to the attention of the Jockey Club!"

The Marchioness sighed again.

"We have been through all this before Lionel, and I do not think for one moment that the Duke intended to do anything that was incorrect."

"That may be your opinion, but it is not mine!" the Marquess said disagreeably.

He was thinking as he spoke that it was not the first time that the Duke had 'pipped him at the post' when he had been quite confident of victory. His horse had been the favourite. He found it hard to acknowledge that an animal from the Strathvegon stables was better than his own. His niece Yseulta put a plate of haddock down in front of him. As if he was determined to find fault with someone, he said,

"That is far too big a helping! I dislike my food being given to me as if it was a dog's dinner!"

Yseulta picked up the plate hastily.

"I am sorry, Uncle Lionel, but yesterday you told me I gave you too little."

"Do not argue with me!" the Marquess roared. "Take away at least half of what you have put on my plate."

Yseulta did as she was told and her uncle watched her, glaring at her as she did so. She was small and very lovely, and it was strange that he should look at her so ferociously. But there was no mistaking the expression of dislike in his eyes as she put the plate down in front of him again. As she sat down at the table he said,

"I shall have some letters for you to take down as soon as I have finished breakfast, and mind they are written better than they were yesterday!"

Yseulta did not answer, and merely bent her head.

She realised as she did so that because of the way her uncle roared at her she no longer felt hungry. In fact it was an effort to eat. Breakfast was the only meal that she always had with her relatives. She found herself dreading it every morning and the moment when her uncle would come into the room and invariably find fault with her.

Now they were in London and as there were usually people to luncheon or dinner, she fortunately did not often come in contact with her uncle again for the rest of the day. Breakfast, she thought privately, was always a purgatory. Although she told herself she was stupid to be upset, she would find herself trembling before she entered the breakfast room. Now the Marquess, still glaring at her, said,

"There were at least three mistakes in the letters you wrote yesterday..."

"Lionel," the Marchioness interrupted, "the groom is waiting, and I think you should open the note and see what it contains."

"It is a pity I cannot even have my breakfast in peace!" the Marquess complained.

Nevertheless he picked up the envelope and slit it open with a knife. He drew out a sheet of writing paper, which was embellished with the Strategus crest. Then he deliberately paused to drink a little coffee before he read the note slowly. As he did so the expression on his face darkened until the Marchioness, who was looking at him apprehensively, asked,

"What is it, Lionel? Who has written to you?"

"Elizabeth Strathvegon," the Marquess replied, "and if you ask me, it is a *damned* insult."

"Really, Lionel, you should not speak like that in front of the girls!" the Marchioness reproved. "Why is it an insult? What does Elizabeth say?"

"Your friend," the Marquess replied, accentuating the adjective, "has invited Sarah to travel to Scotland with her tomorrow, to save her son's face. He has got himself into an unpleasant position from which I sincerely hope he will be unable to escape!"

"What are you talking about?" the Marchioness enquired, "and why should Elizabeth ask Sarah to Scotland in the middle of the Season?"

"I can hardly credit the Duchess expects me to believe this load of nonsense!" the Marquess retorted angrily.

"Please, Lionel," his wife said patiently, "explain what all this is about. It is all incomprehensible to me."

"Well, it is not to me," the Marquess said. "Strathvegon has made a fool of himself, as everybody knows, chasing Hermione Wallington and getting her talked about in the clubs in a manner as disrespectful as if she was a Pretty Horse-Breaker!"

The Marchioness put up her hands.

"Really Lionel, in front of the girls! They should not know about such women!"

"They have got eyes in their heads, I suppose?" the Marquess retorted. "Unless they are blind, they cannot help seeing those 'Bits o' Muslin' disporting themselves in Rotten Row as if they were goddesses instead of strumpets!"

The Marchioness sighed. She knew it was impossible to remonstrate with her husband when he was in one of his rages, but Lady Sarah appeared not in the least shocked as she asked,

"Did you say, Papa, that the Duchess has invited me to go to Scotland? I would love to see Strathvegon Castle. I believe it is magnificent!"

"She has asked you to go to Scotland," the Marquess said, "so that you can become engaged to her badly behaved, raffish son, and save him from the rightful wrath of the Earl of Wallington, who happens to be a friend of mine!"

Before Lady Sarah could reply, the Marquess brought his clenched fist down hard on the breakfast table, so that the cups all rattled.

"I will not allow a daughter of mine to marry Strathvegon," he declared, "and I consider it an insult that she should be asked to do so."

"He has not asked her yet, Lionel," the Marchioness pointed out, "but only to stay in Scotland."

"And why has the Duchess invited her," the Marquess replied aggressively, "except to save her son's skin? She is going to push him up the aisle with any girl who is too half-witted to realise why he is marrying her."

Once again he brought his fist down on the table as he added,

"I would rather see any child of mine in her grave than married to that scoundrel!"

"Now, Lionel, do not upset yourself," the Marchioness begged. "Sarah cannot possibly go to Scotland the day after tomorrow, even if she wanted to. We have a dinner party that night, as well you know."

She paused and as her husband did not speak went on,

"There is the ball being given by the Duchess of Bedford on Saturday, and we have promised to luncheon with the ambassador at the Spanish Embassy on Sunday."

She paused for breath before she added,

"Besides all this there are various other engagements I could not possibly cancel at the last moment."

"I would not allow you to do so," the Marquess retorted, "and I still think it is an unforgivable insult that Strathvegon should think I am so blind as not to see what he is up to."

"There is no point in saying so," the Marchioness said quietly. "Just write and refuse the Duchess's invitation – or would you like Yseulta to do it for you?"

"Yseulta can do it," the Marquess said sharply, "although I expect as usual she will make a mess of it."

Yseulta knew this was unfair, but she was used to her uncle finding fault with everything she did. She therefore rose to her feet and put out her hand to take the note from him. As she did so, the sunshine coming through the window made the very fair hair that framed her small thin face glimmer like a light. Her eyes seemed for the moment to sparkle with the clearness of a mountain stream. To anybody else Yseulta would have looked breathtakingly lovely.

Yet for the Marquess her appearance only accentuated the scowl on his forehead and the hatred in his eyes. Even the plain black gown Yseulta was wearing could not hide the slimness of her figure or the grace with which she moved. As he glanced at the hand she held out for the letter, the sight of her long slim fingers, which looked like those painted so brilliantly by Van Dyck seemed to deepen his anger.

"Here it is!" he said passing her the letter. "And try to write like a lady not a kitchen maid."

As Yseulta took the letter from him he gave a sudden exclamation.

"Wait! I have an idea and, by God, it is a good one!"

"What is it, dear?" the Marchioness asked.

The Marquess hesitated for a moment.

Then he said to Yseulta,

"Go and tell the groom that the Marquess of Derroncorde has received Her Grace's invitation and has much pleasure in accepting it."

What the Marquess said was so surprising that all three women stared at him.

Before his wife could speak the Marquess said to Yseulta,

"Go on! Do as you are told, and do not waste time!"

"Yes, Uncle Lionel," Yseulta replied.

She went from the room.

As if she was bored by a conversation which no longer concerned her, Lady Sarah, who had nearly finished her breakfast before her father had arrived, followed her. As the door shut behind her, the Marchioness said,

"Now, Lionel, what is all this about? It is quite impossible for Sarah to go to Scotland."

"I am aware of that," the Marquess replied, "and Sarah is not going to Scotland, nor would I allow her to set foot in any house owned by the Duke of Strathvegon!"

The Marchioness stared at him.

"Then – why have you accepted?"

"I have accepted verbally the Duchess's invitation," the Marquess explained, "but Sarah is not going to be at King's Cross at noon tomorrow. Instead, I am sending Yseulta!"

The Marchioness's eyes widened in disbelief.

"Yseulta?" she repeated. "But Yseulta cannot possibly go to Scotland. You said yourself she is never to appear anywhere or meet any of our friends!"

"Strathvegon is not my friend!" the Marquess corrected. "He is a man I dislike and distrust. However, I feel he is sharp enough to understand when I repay his insult in an even more insulting manner!"

"By sending Yseulta!" the Marchioness queried.

"Of course!" The Marquess replied. "He is not a fool. He will know exactly what I mean when I suggest by her very appearance that she is exactly the right bride for him. What is more, I shall put it in writing!"

"But, Lionel, you cannot do such a thing!" the Marchioness expostulated. "What would people think if they heard about it?"

The Marquess laughed grimly.

"They will only think that I have cut Strathvegon down to size, which is what I intend to do."

"But how can Yseulta go to Scotland to attend a ball?" the Marchioness enquired. "Apart from anything else, as you refuse to buy her any clothes she has hardly a rag to her back!"

"She is not going to the ball," the Marquess said. "She is merely going to the train with a letter to explain, in case the Duke is too dense to understand what I am insinuating, that she seems to be the only possible person in my household whom I consider lowly enough to associate with him!"

"But surely that is very hard on Yseulta?" the Marchioness suggested.

"All Yseulta will have to do is to present herself as a substitute for Sarah," the Marquess said. "When Strathvegon reads my letter, he will send her straight back here."

He thought for a moment. Then he said,

"Nevertheless, Yseulta will take what she possesses with her, just to make it more uncomfortable for the Duke and his mother to refuse to accept her as their guest."

There was a twisted smile on the Marquess's lips as he said,

"I only wish I could be there to see their reaction when they read what I intend to write. It will make them send Yseulta and her belongings away as if she was a pariah dog. Which, of course, is what she is!"

"Oh, Lionel, it is not the child's fault that her father behaved in such an appalling manner."

"The Bible says, 'The sins of the fathers shall be visited upon the children.'" the Marquess quoted, "and as far as I am concerned, Yseulta will pay for her father's sins until the day I die!"

The Marchioness knew there was no point in arguing. She had already heard this a thousand times before.

She merely sighed again and rising from her chair said,

"I hope you know what you are doing. I have always been very fond of Elizabeth, and I really have no wish to become embroiled in your quarrels with her son."

"You know exactly what I think about him," the Marquess said, "and, as I have told you before, I will not have him in this house!"

"I have no intention of inviting him," the Marchioness said. "There are plenty of decent young men for Sarah to choose from without presenting you with a son-in-law which would make every meal a battlefield!"

"I would not have Strathvegon as my son-in-law if he was the King of England!" the Marquess roared. "I only hope that, as I suspect, George Wallington realises what is going on and fills him so full of lead that he can no longer be a menace to any man who has a pretty wife."

The Marchioness did not bother to reply.

She merely went out of the breakfast room leaving the Marquess to finish what was on his plate and to help himself to more of the haddock he had sent away in the first place. As he sat down again he was thinking of what he would put in the letter that Yseulta was to carry to the Duke. The Duke, whom he detested, would learn exactly what gentlemen like himself thought of him.

*

Yseulta, having given her uncle's message to the groom, went to his study where she knew he would come when he had finished his breakfast. She knew she could expect an hour of sheer torture. He would shout at her, scold her, and occasionally, when he worked himself up into one of his furies, hit her.

At night, when the bruises he had inflicted on her ached, she would lie in the darkness wondering if she had the courage to kill herself as her father had done.

'How can I go on like this, Papa?' she would ask him. 'If I were with you and Mama, I could be happy again as I was when you were both alive.'

Then the tears would come, and although she told herself it was useless, she would cry herself to sleep. It was impossible not to think, almost every minute of the day, of how happy she had been until her father died. They had lived in a small house in Worcestershire. They had very little money because Lord John, being the younger brother of the Marquess, was only given a small allowance. Her mother had nothing because her family was very poor. But Lord John had married for love, and he and his wife were ecstatically happy. He was not in the least envious of his brother who had inherited the title, the estates and all that went with it.

When Yseulta was born her parents were thrilled and adored her. It was only when she grew older that Yseulta realised that her father had deeply offended his family by marrying as he did. His wife was a Scottish girl who was penniless, when he might have married a rich woman. There had been an heiress who had made it clear what she felt about him and the family had rubbed their hands together with delight.

It was providential they thought, that John, who was so handsome, had at twenty-three found somebody so rich. The heiress had been willing, because she loved him, to be content with what was a small title compared to those to which she might have aspired.

The Corde family could therefore hardly believe it possible when John, returning from the North where he had been grouse-shooting with friends, brought with him a *fiancée* who had no money.

Moreover although Iona belonged to a famous clan, she had no social pretentions whatever. That was the beginning of Lord John being in the "black books" of all his Corde relations. They had predicted, and accurately as it turned out, that he would "Come to a bad end".

Lord John and his wife were perfectly happy in the first years of their married life in their small, attractive black and white house in Worcestershire. Lord John had an instinct for training horses, and because he not only rode them extremely well, but he was also able, once they were broken in, to sell them for good prices.

He and his wife, and later his daughter, hunted in the winter. In Summer they grew strawberries in their small garden, boated on the River Avon, and found a great deal to laugh about.

Yseulta, whose name had been chosen by her mother because it was Celtic, was an entrancing baby. At fifteen, when her mother died, she was already very lovely. She was however quite unable to cope with her father's misery at losing his wife.

He had not only loved Iona, but she had become so much a part of himself that without her he was completely lost. He could not bear to be in the house without her and went to London to try to forget, which proved disastrous. He had a great number of friends he had known in his youth and during the short time he had served in the family Regiment, which was the Grenadiers.

They were all very much richer than he was, and soon he found he had spent every penny he possessed and his debts were mounting out of control. Then for a while his luck changed and he bought two horses, which were outstanding. One of them, named St. Vincent, turned out so well that he won several races with him. But what he won in prize-money was a mere 'drop in the ocean' beside the debts he owed.

Then, just before a big race was to take place at Epsom, he was faced by his creditors with a demand that boiled down to "Either payment, or prison."

"What am I to do, Yseulta?" he asked his daughter despairingly.

"I cannot think, Papa," she replied. "For even if St. Vincent wins the race, the prize money will not be enough to pay a quarter of your bills!"

"I know, I know," Lord John said despairingly.

"The trouble is," Yseulta said, "St. Vincent is already the favourite and odds on. Which means that he will not be worth backing."

Because she loved her father, she understood everything about racing. She knew that as a rule he would never have thought of backing his own horses. But what she had said unfortunately gave Lord John an idea. The other horse he had bought with St. Vincent, which was called Dark Cloud, was its full brother by the same mare and sired by the same stallion.

They were almost identical except that St. Vincent had a white star on his forehead.

It was a race in which the owners, if they were young enough and healthy enough, could ride their own horses. Lord John had announced that he was riding St. Vincent – but at the last moment he switched to Dark Cloud.

No one watching the horses in the paddock had the slightest idea that Dark Cloud was not the favourite. In a desperate gamble to save himself and his home, Lord John had painted a white star on Dark Cloud and dyed St. Vincent's star to match the rest of his coat.

There was not a great deal of interest in the race until they were half-way round the course. Then, to everybody's astonishment, a comparatively unknown horse was in the lead. As 'Dark Cloud' romped home two lengths ahead of the field there was a gasp of astonishment from the spectators.

As Lord John rode up to the weighing-in-room he was smiling. Everybody was congratulating him and exclaiming in surprise that an unknown horse had done so well. It was then that a very lovely lady with whom he had spent some time in London exclaimed petulantly,

"Oh, John, look what your horse has done to my gloves! And they were a new pair!"

She held up her long white suede gloves as she spoke, everyone around could see they were streaked with a brown dye. Confusion followed. Suddenly it was found that Lord John had disappeared although nobody had noticed him go. He was found later that evening dead in his lodgings in Half Moon Street. He had shot himself through the head and died instantly.

Yseulta was orphaned, penniless, alone and feeling desperate when her uncle came to the house in Worcestershire.

"Your father has defamed the family name," he said, "and I am ashamed and disgusted that I should have a crook and a cheat for a brother! As you have nowhere to go and are too old to be placed in an orphanage, I shall have to take you into my home."

His voice sharpened and he roared at her,

"But I loathe and detest you because you are my brother's child and he has betrayed me!"

He had taken Yseulta back with him to the Cordes' ancestral house in Berkshire. There she found herself treated as a scapegoat for her father's sins, which she was never allowed to forget.

She was slave to her Cousin Sarah and her uncle employed her as his secretary. He already had one, but because he wished to abuse her, he insisted that a lot of his correspondence was done by her.

He refused to buy her any more clothes and she wore the black she had bought when her mother died until the gowns were in rags. Only when a garment was completely unwearable or indecent was it replaced by her aunt. But again in black, so that her uncle would be unaware that she had anything new to wear.

She moved about the house like a ghost, keeping out of sight when anybody came, being with the family only when they were alone. She felt sometimes she would have become mentally unstable if it had not been for the library. Because it was so large, the Marquess had no idea how many of the books she borrowed and read before she went to sleep. If he had, he would undoubtedly have stopped her from taking them.

The servants despised her, as servants always despise an underling who incurs the wrath of their master. It was a life she had now endured for nearly two years.

At eighteen, when Sarah was making her debut and attending balls every night, Yseulta had nothing to look forward to but misery and despair. When she came back from speaking to the groom as her uncle had told her to do, she thought wistfully how wonderful it would be if she could go to Scotland. Her mother had so often described it to her and she had searched in the library for pictures of the moors, the mountains and the lochs.

Then as she reached the study she found that her uncle was already there, and she felt herself tremble. She knew, because he was already in a rage, that he would be more aggressive than he usually was. He would doubtless hit her if she failed to please him, which anyway it was impossible for her to do.

CHAPTER THREE

The Duke, trotting his horse in Rotten Row, saw Hermione Wallington in the distance and stopped to talk to a lovely lady in a carriage. He made himself very pleasant, so that its occupant blushed coyly and flirted with him under her eyelashes in a provocative manner. Before he rode away she had begged him to call on her whenever he was free, and the way he responded was very encouraging.

He then rode on to where Hermione, looking ravishingly beautiful in a blue habit that matched the colour of her eyes, was talking to two of his friends. He rode up to them, raising his hat, and said in an enthusiastic voice,

"Good morning, Countess! I hope you have recovered from the boredom of the party last night. I saw you were sitting next to the Archbishop of Canterbury, and my heart bled for you!"

To his relief, after one frantic glance, which he thought was indiscreet, Hermione replied,

"I always find those state occasions tedious, except that they are so picturesque in that beautiful dining room!"

"You mean *you* are!" one of the gentlemen beside her remarked gallantly.

She smiled very prettily at the compliment. Because the two gentlemen who had been entertaining her were tactful and admitted that the Duke had a prior claim, they moved off. The Duke and Hermione rode slowly in the opposite direction, and he said quickly,

"I talked to my mother last night and we are leaving for Scotland tomorrow morning before your husband arrives."

Hermione gave a gasp as he had expected she would. But before she could expostulate he said,

"You must be aware it is the only thing I can do, and my mother is giving a ball at the castle, which will be our excuse for leaving so precipitately."

He did not tell her that his mother had persuaded him he must announce his engagement. He knew that if he did so it was very likely, as Hermione had so little self-control, that she would either scream or burst into tears. He was quite certain they were being watched by everybody in that part of the Row.

At last, with an effort to speak calmly, she said,

"I must see you before you go. You cannot ... leave me like this!"

"The difficulty is – where?" the Duke replied.

Hermione thought for a moment. Then she said,

"Why not the Grosvenor Chapel? If we go up on the balcony, nobody will notice us."

The Duke was astonished. It would never have entered his mind to meet any of the women with whom he was involved in a church.

"You can walk there," Hermione went on, "but my coachman will not be surprised if I stop to say a prayer as I have done before."

This made the Duke aware that this was not the first time she had met a lover in such a strange place. He thought actually that it was unexpectedly intelligent of her.

"At what time?" he asked as he saw another of his friends looming down on them.

"Four o'clock," she whispered.

There was no chance of saying any more. The Duke's friend greeted him jovially and paid Hermione several gushing compliments. After a short discussion the Duke took his gold watch out of his pocket and said,

"I am afraid I must leave you. I have an appointment at eleven o'clock with my manager from the country. I am sure it means a doleful tale or urgent repairs to buildings and expenditure on a great many things that apparently eat money as if it was grass!"

His friend laughed.

"Landowners always complain," he said, "but nobody is going to feel sorry for you, Strathvegon. By the way, how are the grouse doing this year?"

"They hatched out in excellent weather," the Duke answered. "But I will be able to tell you more next week, after I return."

"Return?" his friend repeated. "You are going to Scotland?"

"I have to," the Duke replied. "My mother is giving a ball at the castle, and she insists on my being present."

"Well, do not stay away for too long," his friend remarked. "We shall miss you."

"I shall return as soon as it is possible," the Duke replied.

He looked at Hermione as he spoke and saw the anguish in her eyes. Quickly, in case she betrayed herself, he swept his hat off with a courtly gesture.

"Au revoir, Countess," he said. "I am sorry we shall not meet at the Bedford Ball. I let the Duchess know this morning that I am unfortunately unable to attend her dinner party."

Hermione managed to smile at him but he saw the tears were not far from her eyes. Quickly he rode away, waving to one or two friends as he went. He rode back to Strathvegon House and found his mother, as he expected, downstairs in the Morning Room. He kissed her and she said,

"Everything is arranged, Kenyon. I have sent Mr. Watson to Scotland with the invitations for the ball, which will be distributed as soon as he arrives."

She paused, and as the Duke did not speak, she went on,

"I have ordered your private train to be at King's Cross, I think it is Platform 7, by eleven o'clock tomorrow morning so that the servants can have everything in order before we arrive."

"You have been very busy!" the Duke said in a somewhat sulky voice.

"I have had to be dearest," his mother said, "and here is the list of people who are coming with us."

She handed him the list, which included two of her closest friends and their husbands, who were always ready to do anything she asked of them. There were also three young men who she knew were close friends of his and had been so ever since they had been at school together.

At the bottom of the list there were the names of three girls, Lady Beryl Wood, Lady Deborah Hurst, and Lady Sarah Corde. The Duke read their names slowly, knowing he had not the slightest idea what any of them looked like. He had always been careful never to become involved in any way with unmarried girls. He knew how easy it was for an ambitious mother to ensnare a desirable suitor so that there was no escape.

One of his closest friends, Lord Worcester, had been forced into marriage because the girl's mother had seen him talking to her alone in the garden. They had met there entirely by chance, but the mother had appealed to the Princess of Wales. She claimed that her daughter's reputation would be ruined if she was talked about as having been alone with a young man.

Under pressure from both the Princess and the Prince, there was nothing Lord Worcester could do but propose marriage. He then accepted with as much grace as he could muster the congratulations of his friends. The Duke had enjoyed a great many *affairs de coeur,* in fact they teased him in the clubs as being a 'Casanova'.

It was impossible to deny that he had flitted from flower to flower, discarding one beauty after another. The difficulty was, and he admitted it himself now, that he was easily bored. Once the lady of the moment had surrendered herself and inevitably, it seemed, given him her heart, he began to find their love-making somewhat monotonous. Similarly her conversation, which concerned one subject, and one subject only, became incredibly boring.

It was perhaps this, more than anything else, that made him reject every plea for his mother that he should marry. On his thirty-second birthday she talked to him seriously about producing an heir.

"Do you realise, my darling," she said, "that if you do not produce a son, your uncle, whom you have never liked, and neither do I for that matter, will take your place as head of the clan? And he has no son to succeed him."

"That is undoubtedly true," the Duke agreed.

He knew his uncle had produced five daughters from two marriages and was doubtless still trying to produce a son and heir. But the Duke had said finally to his mother,

"It is no use Mama, I cannot for the moment contemplate being tied to some young woman who will make me yawn every time she opens her mouth. The women I find most attractive are, as you know, already married."

"I know," the Duchess agreed, "and I want you to be happy. At the same time, it would be so wonderful for me to hold my grandson in my arms and know he is exactly like you were as a baby."

"There is plenty of time," the Duke had said hastily, "and I promise you I will consider marriage very seriously when I reach middle age!"

Before the Duchess could expostulate that that was far too long to wait, the Duke had prevented the words from leaving her lips by saying,

"I must leave you, Mama. Somebody very alluring with eyes like emeralds, for which she has an inexhaustible desire, is waiting for me."

Because the Duchess found her son incorrigible and in fact knew the beauty in question, she laughed. Before she could say any more the Duke had left her. Looking at the list that he held in his hand the Duke guessed that each of the girls whom his mother had picked as a prospective bride were young, gauche and doubtless badly educated.

He had seen their like all too often when his friends had been married one after the other, and at least half-a-dozen weddings he had acted as Best Man. He had to admit however that there was one thing about them that was extraordinary. After they had retired to the country for several years and produced a son and perhaps two or three other children, they emerged as the beautiful, witty, sophisticated women that he found so attractive.

It was difficult to understand how the transformation took place. But there was no doubt that it did, and he supposed now that even Hermione had once been shy and rather clumsy. He admitted to himself that if he had married her when she was a debutante he would long before now have been looking for what was called 'another interest'.

He handed the list back to his mother.

"I suppose there is no other way out?" he asked.

"If there is, I cannot think of it," the Duchess replied, "and I remembered in the night that five years ago George Wallington wounded a man so badly that he had to have his arm amputated."

"I had no idea of that!" the Duke exclaimed.

"I think you were abroad at the time," the Duchess replied, "and anyway, as the man in question was of no particular consequence, it was all hushed up and quickly forgotten."

She gave a little shudder as she said,

"I could not bear it, Kenyon dearest, that anything like that should happen to you!"

The Duke walked away to stand at the window, looking out with unseeing eyes onto the garden at the back of the house.

"Which of these unfledged chits do you favour?" he enquired in a hard voice.

There was silence before the Duchess answered,

"Beryl Wood is, I think, the most beautiful. She is dark, which you might find rather alluring."

The Duke knew she was referring to the fact that Hermione had golden hair of which was inordinately proud. She was invariably referred to as being 'An English Rose'.

"Deborah Hurst is not so beautiful," the Duchess went on, "but I believe has rather a jolly character, and

Sarah Corde has red hair like her mother, who is a very old friend of mine."

"In other words, you favour Sarah Corde," the Duke said in an uncompromising voice.

"I have a feeling the Marquess does not like you," the Duchess said, "but that is because your horses invariably beat his, and as he is a conceited man, he resents it!"

The Duke smiled.

"He was certainly furious at Epsom last week when my horse beat his by a nose!"

"Then you must always be diplomatic in the future and not enter your horses for the races that he particularly wants to win."

"I am quite prepared to do even that rather than marry his daughter!" the Duke said almost as if he spoke to himself.

The Duchess rose from her writing table to walk to the window and slip her arm through her son's.

"I am sorry darling about this," she said, "but you know I will do anything to make things as easy for you as possible."

"I know Mama, and I am grateful," the Duke replied. "At the same time, I have no wish to marry anyone and certainly not some idiotic schoolgirl with whom I have absolutely nothing in common!"

The Duchess sighed but she did not reply and the Duke suddenly swore in a furious tone,

"*Damn Wallington!* How dare he threaten me and make his wife utterly miserable!"

"I think actually," the Duchess said, "he loves Hermione, and men when they are in love are often unrestrained and what you would think to be unreasonable."

She was not sure the Duke was listening but she went on,

"The truth is, my beloved son, you have never been in love. When you are, you will understand what I am talking about."

She walked away leaving the room as she spoke, and the Duke looked after her in astonishment.

'Never been in love?' he said to himself. 'What the devil does she mean by that!'

He thought of how many times he had been enthralled, fascinated, totally captivated by a lovely face and a perfectly curved body. He thought of the nights when he had seemed to touch the heights of passion and the innumerable dawns when he had walked home, his head in the clouds. Never been in love?

Good Heavens, what did his mother think he was feeling now about Hermione? Then what seemed like a voice from within him asked cynically,

'Do you really think that what you feel for her will last? Would you really be content to have her with you day and night for the rest of your life?'

It was a question he did not want to answer. He went from the room to order his chaise to be brought round immediately. Because he was still playing the part for which he felt he had written the script, he drove to White's.

He had luncheon with three of his closest friends who happened to have no other invitations that day. He placed several bets on the racing taking place at Doncaster that afternoon. Afterwards he went to Bond Street to buy a present for Hermione and told himself bitterly it was a farewell present to freedom.

He knew he dare not give her anything that could be used as incriminating evidence by her husband. He therefore chose a handle for a sunshade, which was extremely expensive, but which he hoped would escape George Wallington's jealous eyes. Of pink quartz, it was encircled with turquoises and small diamonds. The Duke hesitated over whether it should be engraved with her initials, then decided it would be a mistake. Instead he had it packed up and took it with him.

He returned home, sent his chaise away and ten minutes later walked into the hall.

"You're going out, Your Grace?" the butler asked in surprise. "Shall I send to the stables for a conveyance?"

"No, thank you," the Duke replied. "I intend to walk. I need the exercise and it is a nice afternoon."

"It is a trifle warm, but as Your Grace says, a nice day."

The Duke walked into Park Lane, then took the first turning which led him to South Audley Street where the Grosvenor Chapel was situated. He was wise enough to arrive early so that Hermione's servants, when they conveyed her to the chapel, would not see him.

As he expected, there was no one at this hour of the day in the chapel and he climbed up the stairs that led to the balcony. He thought only a woman would have suggested a church as a good place for an assignation with her lover. He sat at the back of the balcony where he realised he could not be seen by anybody below.

He could just see the altar and the stained-glass windows above it. When he was in Scotland he went to the kirk because it was expected of him, and it was something his father had always done. He knew that the Minister expected to see a member of the family sitting in the big carved pew that had been there since the kirk was first built. He had attended some churches in London either for a wedding service at which he was an important guest, or for a funeral at which he was a mourner.

He found himself thinking, not of Hermione as might have been expected, but of what he had believed when he was a little boy. His mother had read him the story of Bethlehem and it had excited him. Then he had imagined himself riding in the desert with the Three Wise Men as they followed the star. He thought somewhat cynically that he had followed a great many stars since then. But they had never led him to what he really sought, whatever that might be.

As he was puzzling as to where his thoughts were leading him, Hermione arrived. She had come so softly up the stairs that he had not heard her. She moved swiftly towards him with her hands outstretched.

Her eyes beneath the brim of her very becoming bonnet were alight because he was there. He raised her hands one after the other to his lips and as they sat down she said in a whisper,

"Oh, Kenyon are you really going to Scotland? How can I lose you and have to face George all on my own?"

"My mother assures me it is the only possible thing I can do for both our sakes," the Duke replied, "and you have to be brave."

"I am trying to be," Hermione said, "but I am frightened, very frightened! And Jones thinks she knows who has been watching us."

"Who is it?" the Duke asked sharply.

He was half-afraid that the Earl might have employed an agency, in which case there was always the danger that he and Hermione could be blackmailed.

"Jones thinks," Hermione was saying, "that it is his secretary, Mr. Marsden, a man I have never liked, who has not been with George for very long. He sucks up to him in a nauseating manner."

She made a little gesture with her hands before she said,

"I am quite certain he thinks he is ingratiating himself with George by watching us as I am sure he asked him to do."

The Duke was thinking that if Hermione was right, and the Earl's secretary was watching them, the evidence he must have accumulated would be very incriminating. Too late, he thought. He must have been mad to have made love to Hermione in her own house. In fact it was something he had always disliked doing. He had no wish to eat the food, drink the wine, or use the bed of a man whose wife was being unfaithful.

But inevitably there was no alternative. For a lady to come to his house was unthinkable. If anyone had the least idea she had done so, it would brand her immediately as a 'Scarlet Woman'.

In all the *affairs de coeur* in London there was always the pretence that paid lip service to the conventions. It was quite permissible for a married woman to give a small dinner party in her husband's absence. After all, he could hardly expect her to sit at home alone when he was away.

The guests, perhaps four of them, were chosen with care. When they left, if they were tactful, soon after dinner, one of the gentlemen would stay behind ostensibly to go on talking to his hostess. An obliging lady's maid, like Jones, would also go to bed, leaving her mistress's bedroom ready but unattended. There would then be nobody except perhaps a sleepy night-footman to know what time a lover left. His silence could be bought by a few gold sovereigns pressed into his hand.

It had always seemed to the Duke that it was all uncomplicated and very civilised. Now as he thought of the Earl's secretary waiting in the shadows, with a watch in his hand and a notebook in which to record dates and times, he realised he had been a fool.

'I might have known,' he thought, 'that sooner or later somebody like George Wallington would be suspicious and determined to find out the truth.'

There were always of course a convenient number of complacent husbands who deliberately shut their eyes and plugged their ears. They were themselves usually occupied with 'another interest' and therefore unconcerned with what their wives were doing. It struck the Duke, as if for the first time, that if he was married he would very much resent his wife taking a lover in his absence. Suddenly he understood Wallington's fury at being cuckolded.

"When shall I see you again?" Hermione was asking.

The Duke's fingers tightened on hers as he said,

"I think I should tell you the truth."

"What is that?" Hermione asked.

"My mother intends to announce my engagement at the ball she is giving next week!"

Hermione stared at him as if she could not believe what she had heard.

The she put her hand up to her lips as if to stifle a scream.

"I do not believe it! It cannot be ... true!" she cried.

"My mother feels it is the only way we can prevent your husband from divorcing you and calling me out."

"But, who will you marry? Why have you never spoken of her?"

"I have never spoken of her," the Duke explained, "because I have never met her!"

"I-I do not understand," Hermione said.

"My mother has invited a house party to stay at the castle, and among them are three girls whom she has chosen as suitable to be my wife."

His voice hardened as he spoke. Even Hermione, her eyes filled with unshed tears, realised how much he disliked the idea.

"Oh, Kenyon ... how can I bear it?" she asked.

He did not speak, and after a moment she said in a different voice,

"Of course, now I think of it, it may make things easier for us."

"Easier?" the Duke asked.

"If you are marrying somebody, then George cannot go on being suspicious, and when you come back..."

There was no need for her to say any more. The Duke felt a sudden revulsion against an idea that he knew would make him feel even more despicable than he did already. It was bad enough in all conscience to have to marry a girl cold-bloodedly. He was doing it in order to save himself from being shot at by Wallington and cited as co-respondent in a divorce case. But to plan adultery before the ring was even on the girl's finger, struck him as being in such bad taste that he wished to have no part of it.

"I think, Hermione, we must say goodbye to each other now," he said at last. "Your servants will think it odd if you stay too long and may come to investigate."

Hermione stiffened and looked over her shoulder as if she thought somebody might have come up the stairs without her being aware of it. Then she said,

"Oh dearest, wonderful Kenyon, I love you with all my heart, and I can only pray that we will be together again and it will not be too long before that happens."

The way she spoke made the Duke suspect that it was a little speech she had thought out before she came to the chapel. She moved a little nearer to him, lifting her lips to his.

For a moment he hesitated. It seemed wrong somehow to be kissing in the chapel. Then because he could not refuse her, he kissed her lips very gently, without passion.

"Goodbye, my beautiful one," he said, "and thank you for all the happiness you have given me."

He put the present he had bought her, and which he had set down on the chair next to him, into her hand. As she looked at it curiously he said,

"When you use it, think of me, as I shall be thinking of you."

"Oh, Kenyon, I love you, and I shall never love anyone else in the ... same way," Hermione said brokenly.

She rose to her feet and as the Duke rose too, she kissed him again, her lips lingering hungrily on his. Then with a little sob she turned away and without looking back walked from the balcony down the staircase that led to the entrance to the chapel.

The Duke stood, until he heard the door close behind her. Then he sat down and stared at the stained-glass window over the altar. He was thinking as he did so, that he was paying a heavy price for what he had called "the happiness" that Hermione had given him.

He thought of the Earl's secretary watching him come and go and sending a report to his master in Paris, which he was well-aware would be a catastrophe for the Countess.

'*Damn him! He* deserves to be shot!' the Duke thought.

He told himself angrily that the one thing in life he hated was stupidity. But nothing could have been more stupid than the way that he had assumed himself to be safe from spies and informers.

He had in consequence put a rope not only around his own neck, but also around Hermione's. He had the feeling, however, that she would be able to talk herself out of trouble. There was no doubt that her husband was still infatuated with her. If he had so much as looked at another woman, the gossips would certainly have chatted about it. If for no other reason, they would have done so to humiliate Hermione, because they were so jealous of her beauty.

No, Hermione would be safe, the Duke decided, but he would pay the price, and it was a very heavy one. He would receive a life sentence.

When he was quite certain there would be no one to notice him, he walked out of the chapel and hurried back to Strathvegon House.

He was wondering what he should do with himself this evening. He had previously arranged to dine with Hermione as he had before and to spend one last wild night of love with her before her husband returned from Paris.

He was wondering whether he should go to the club or ask some of his friends to dine with him. He had the feeling that might be a mistake as they would think it strange that he was not with Hermione as they expected. He was quite certain now, although he had never thought of it before, that it was not only Wallington's secretary who would check him in and out, but quite a number of other people as well.

'Damn it!' he said to himself. 'Is there no way a man can have privacy?'

He handed his hat to a footman who said,

"Her Grace wishes to see you, Your Grace, the moment you return."

The Duke thought that his mother would be in the drawing room where she usually had tea at this hour. He walked up the stairs to find her, as he expected, sitting in one of the windows enjoying the sunshine. To his relief she was alone.

"Ah, here you are darling!" she exclaimed. "Let me pour you a cup of tea and I will tell you what I have planned for the evening."

"Planned for the evening?" the Duke questioned, conscious that he was repeating the words rather stupidly.

"I thought," the Duchess explained, "that as you were likely to be free, I would ask several of our friends to dinner and take a box at Drury Lane. We may not get there in time for the first part of what is, I have heard, a very good show, but I am sure you will enjoy it."

There was a twinkle in his mother's eyes as she spoke. The Duke knew quite well that she had planned it so that he would be seen in public. Marsden, or whoever else was watching them, would not be able to report to George Wallington that they had been together this evening.

"Afterwards," the Duchess went on, "I have promised that we will look in at a reception at Apsley House. You may find it a little dull, but the Prime Minister will be there, besides of course, a great number of other statesmen."

The Duke laughed as if he could not help it.

"Mama, you are marvellous!" he said. "I suppose I ought to be grateful, but at the moment I feel more like hitting somebody, preferably myself, for being a fool!"

The Duchess put up her hand.

"We all make mistakes, dearest boy," she said, "and the most important thing is to make certain we do not make the same one a second time!"

CHAPTER FOUR

As the carriage carrying Yseulta drew nearer to King's Cross, she felt more and more frightened.

She had in fact been horrified when her Uncle had said to her,

"Take down this letter and you shall carry it tomorrow to the Duke of Strathvegon."

She had been surprised, knowing how much her uncle disliked the Duke, that he should be writing to him at all. Then when she took down in her elegant handwriting what he dictated, she was astounded.

As she finished what he was saying she exclaimed,

"But surely Uncle…?"

"Shut up!" he roared. "I do not want any arguments from you, and you will do exactly what I tell you to do!"

She was too frightened to say any more, but she lay awake for most of the night wondering how she could endure such humiliation. It was bad enough to have to listen to her father being abused day after day by his relatives. But to have him publicly denounced in front of strangers made her wish she could die, or at least run away and hide. Then morning came and she knew there was nothing she could do but obey her uncle.

She had not a penny piece to call her own, and she had nowhere to go if she left his house. Although she thought to starve to death would be better than to have to endure his insults and cruelty day after day, she had not the courage to attempt it A maid called her noisily at seven o'clock, as was usual, and when she was getting up had come back to say,

"His Lordship's given orders, Miss Yseulta, that you've to pack everything you require in this basket."

She put down on the floor as she spoke a common basket-type piece of luggage that was usually carried by servants. It was in fact the cheapest type of travelling luggage obtainable. When she was alone Yseulta thought that what she had been told to do was a waste of time. She might take her luggage to the train as her uncle had ordered, but when she was sent scornfully away she would only have to bring it back and unpack it again.

It was only when she was travelling towards the station that she began to wonder if it would be possible to hide herself somewhere on the Duke's train. It would carry her to Scotland, and once she was in the Highlands she would disappear, so that her uncle would never find her again. And she was quite certain he would be delighted to be rid of her.

Perhaps there would be people in Scotland who would pay her to scrub their floors or cook their food.

Anything would be preferable to suffering as she had these last two years. Then she knew that even to think of escaping was just a hopeless dream. She would wake up to find herself once again wincing from the blows her uncle inflicted on her.

The carriage drew up at the station and a footman stepped down to pick up her luggage with a disdainful air. She knew that on her uncle's orders he was to take her to the train rather than get her a porter. This was because the Marquess wanted the Duke's friends to see the Derroncorde livery the footman was wearing. He wanted them to be aware who he was, even if the Duke did not enlighten them.

As she walked down the platform she could feel herself trembling and felt as if she was going to the guillotine. At the same time, a pride she had almost forgotten she possessed, made her hold her head high rather than run away and hide. It had crossed her mind in fact to do just that. Then, when the train had left the station, to return and tell her uncle she had been too late to see the Duke. She was aware that it was already twelve o'clock. Her uncle was making sure that the rest of the party would have already arrived. They were to be the audience of the scene in which he intended her to be involved.

'How can I face it?' she asked herself.

Every nerve in her body seemed to be on edge. Then she suddenly felt as if her mother was beside her, comforting her and telling her she must be brave. Her chin went higher, and she walked a little slower, as if she would behave with dignity. She saw the train just ahead of her and thought it was in fact very attractive. Painted white, with the window-frames and doors a deep ruby red, it looked almost like a child's toy. As Yseulta reached it she saw the Guard was already waiting, his red flag in his hand, for the Duke's order to leave.

The drawing room car was closest to the engine, while the sleeping compartments were behind. She passed them before she came to where she could see through the windows the brilliantly coloured hats of the Duke's lady guests.

A few men were standing talking to them. She gave them only a fleeting glance – at the same time they made her feel more nervous than she was already. A Scotsman, wearing the kilt in the Duke's tartan, was standing by the steps that led into the drawing room. He looked at Yseulta in surprise.

Inside the drawing room the Duchess had just said to her son,

"Everybody is here except Sarah Corde."

"It is a woman's privilege to be late," the Duke replied. "So I suppose we should give her at least five minutes' grace."

He looked at his watch as he spoke. As the Duchess moved away to speak to one of her friends on the other side of the coach, he saw through the window a strange-looking young woman. She was dressed completely in black, which he could see was not only dowdy but also threadbare. For a moment he thought she must be a lady's maid who had not been shown, as she should have been, into one of the carriages at the rear of the train. Then realised that the woman who was drawing nearer had strangely fair hair that seemed to be haloed by a little black hat she wore on the back of her head.

He had a glimpse of two very large eyes. She reached the coach and he saw her speak to Douglas, his personal servant. He wondered what was happening.

Then he saw that behind the woman in black there was a footman carrying a strange piece of luggage. His liveried waistcoat and tall cockaded hat showed him to be a servant of somebody of importance. It then came to the Duke's mind that this must be Lady Sarah Corde. But he knew she would hardly be dressed in what was obviously deep mourning, if she was, as his mother had said, a debutante enjoying the London Season.

Douglas came into the drawing room and reaching his master's side said, in what the Duke thought was an unusually low voice,

"Miss Yseulta Corde wishes t'speak to Yer Grace."

The woman in black was just behind him, and now the Duke could see that she was very young with two large and very frightened grey eyes. He could not remember when he had ever before seen a woman with such a stricken expression on her face. As he stared at her she came a little nearer and said in a voice he could hardly hear,

"I-I was told Your Grace ... to give this note to you personally."

She held it out to him and he saw that her hand was trembling. He also realised that her black glove was worn and the fingers had been darned in several places. Feeling this was all very strange, he took the note from her as he said,

"I suspect, Miss Corde, you have come to tell me that Lady Sarah is unable to join my party."

She looked more frightened than ever as she said in a voice that trembled,

"W-will you please read ... the note."

The Duke opened the envelope without difficulty, finding it was not very firmly sealed, and drew out the sheet of thick writing paper.

It was folded in two, and opening it he read,

> *'I am well aware of your pathetic efforts to escape from a situation that is of your own contriving. I will not allow my daughter to demean herself by agreeing to act as a 'Lifebelt' to save you from drowning! Instead I have sent you the daughter of my late brother John, whose criminal, disgraceful and treacherous behaviour should make her a fitting partner for you!*

Derroncorde.'

The Duke felt his temper rise.

He stood staring at the note, thinking it was impossible that any man could behave so offensively to him. Then a frightened little voice beside him said,

"I-I am sorry."

"You know what your uncle has written?" the Duke asked.

"H-he made me write it for him."

"And you realise how insulting it is?"

Yseulta drew in her breath, but she did not speak. The Duke thought it impossible for any woman to look so miserable, so piteously unhappy.

"I-I am ... s-sorry," she said again. "I will go away at once."

"Is it what your uncle expected you to do?" the Duke asked.

He saw her glance at his guests, laughing and chattering behind him, as she twisted her fingers together in her shabby gloves. He knew she was expecting him to denounce her loudly so that everybody could hear, then order her to leave his train immediately. He saw how ingeniously the Marquess, who was a big, blustery, loud-voiced man, had thought it out.

He wanted not only to humiliate him, but also this wretched girl who was just a pawn in his hands. The Duke had not spoken again. Yseulta, as if she was breaking under the tension, had half-turned towards the door when the Duchess came to her son's side.

"What is it, Kenyon?" she asked. "What has happened?"

The Duke put the note he had received into the inside pocket of his coat.

"Miss Corde has brought me a note to say that unfortunately Lady Sarah cannot join us," he replied. "But as she does not wish to upset our numbers, she has sent her cousin in her place."

As she spoke Yseulta turned back to stare at him in sheer astonishment.

She was very pale and her eyes seemed to fill her small, oval face.

"But this is delightful!" the Duchess said. "And now that our party is complete, we can be on our way."

She took a step towards Yseulta, saying in her usual sweet manner,

"Come with me, my dear, and let me introduce you to the other members of the party."

For a moment Yseulta could not move. Then she heard the Duke say over her head to Douglas,

"See that Miss Corde's luggage is brought aboard, and then inform the Guard that we are ready to leave."

"Very good, Yer Grace."

Douglas, speaking with a strong Scottish accent, carried out his orders. Almost immediately there was the slamming of doors and the shrill sound of a whistle. Then as the Guard waved his red flag the train began to pull away from the platform.

The Duchess had taken Yseulta to the back of the carriage to where Lady Beryl Wood and Lady Deborah Hurst were sitting with two of the Duke's friends. The Duchess introduced them, explaining that Yseulta had come in her cousin's place. She sat down in a seat near the window feeling as if her whole world had turned upside-down, or else she was asleep and dreaming.

As soon as the train started, stewards had appeared. They carried trays containing small appetisers for the guests to eat while they sipped their champagne from the glasses that had already been handed round.

Because she was bewildered Yseulta accepted a glass of champagne and a piece of *pâté de foie gras* on a small biscuit.

She was hardly aware of what she was doing. Then as the train gathered speed she realised that incredibly her wish had come true, and she was on her way to Scotland. It was then she told herself that she would never go back. However frightening it would be, to be in a strange country and among what might seem to be foreigners – she would be free.

Anything would be better than to go on enduring the cruelty meted out by her uncle. Yesterday, after he had dictated the letter, he had deliberately made her copy it out three times. This was not because there was anything wrong with it, for she had made sure of that. It was because, he said, he wanted to keep one to show his friends, and another for his files.

"I intend," he said, "Never to forget how I have told that scoundrel exactly what I think of him."

When Yseulta had tried to protest against having to take it personally to the Duke, he had hit her not once, but twice. He told her that if she did not obey him, he would beat her until she did.

"Your father has poisoned my name," he raged at her, "And if you disobey me, I will thrash you until you are unconscious – do you understand?"

He shouted so loudly that she felt as if he would break her eardrums. He had been so overbearing and had hurt her so much that she had screamed. When she left him she felt so faint that she had to lie down before she could do anything else. Yet now, incredibly, when she thought the Duke would be even more abusive than her uncle, she was leaving London and was on her way to Scotland!

'Thank You God ... *thank You!'* she said in her heart.

Then she became aware that the people sitting near her were looking at her curiously.

She put her glass of champagne quickly down on a table and ate the *pâté* just in case the wine should make her feel light-headed. She had been unable to eat any breakfast because she was so frightened of what she was being compelled to do.

Yesterday she had felt too sick and upset by her uncle's behaviour to eat anything either at luncheon or dinner.

'I must be careful,' she admonished herself, 'In case I behave badly because I am so excited.'

It was then with difficulty she tried to take an interest in the people around her. She noticed that Lady Deborah Hurst was giggling at everything the gentlemen were saying to her, but that Lady Beryl Wood was only looking sulky. Yet there was nothing, Yseulta felt, to make her feel anything but happy. She was dressed in the most elegant gown with a matching bonnet trimmed with white camellias and green leaves.

The appetisers were followed by a delicious luncheon and, to her surprise, Yseulta found herself eating quite a lot of every course. She realised that several of the Duke's guests were looking at her curiously, but they were too polite and too well bred to do so obviously. The gentlemen, whose names she learned were Hugo, Anthony and Perry, teased the girls and made jokes which, with the exception of Lady Beryl, they thought very funny.

It had been so long since anyone had talked to Yseulta as if she was a human being, that she could hardly believe that what was happening was true. When luncheon was over the party seemed to sort itself out into small groups. The Duchess's friends, the two middle-aged couples, settled down to a game of bridge. Hugo was showing Deborah, who giggled at everything he said, some pictures in a magazine.

The Duchess was consulting Anthony who was, apparently, an expert dancer, as to how many reels they should have at the ball. It was then the Duke came to the back of the coach and sat down on an empty seat next to Yseulta. He was holding a glass of brandy in his hand and he looked across the table and said to Lady Beryl,

"Is there anything I can get you? I noticed you appeared not to enjoy the luncheon as much as my mother had hoped you would."

Lady Beryl looked at him in what Yseulta thought was a hostile manner. Then, to her surprise, Lady Beryl said,

"I want nothing, thank you, except to be left alone."

She rose as she spoke and moved to a chair on the other side of the coach which had been vacated by the bridge players. She settled herself against the window and shut her eyes as if she intended to go to sleep. The Duke, who had watched her in astonishment, turned to Yseulta. They were a little apart from the rest of the group and he said in a low voice,

"Tell me why you are wearing black. Are you in mourning?"

Yseulta shook her head. Then after a little pause she said impulsively,

"It was very, very kind of you not to turn me away as I had expected you would. I promise I will be no trouble to you and when we reach Scotland I will disappear, so that Uncle Lionel can never find me again."

"Why should you do that?" the Duke asked.

"Because I cannot bear to stay with him any longer," Yseulta replied.

Then as if she felt she had been indiscreet and perhaps foolish, she looked up at the Duke and said frantically,

"You will not tell him what I said? You will not make me go back?"

"No, of course not. Why should I if you do not wish to?" the Duke replied. "But you must realise that I am curious to learn why you should feel like that, and why you are wearing black."

Yseulta drew in her breath.

"My … my uncle hates me for what Papa did – but I suppose it is understandable."

She looked away from the Duke before she said in a voice that was almost a whisper,

"I only wish I was brave enough to follow him."

"I remember seeing your father ride," the Duke remarked. "I thought he was magnificent! It was not always because his horse was so good, but that he rode so superbly that he seemed almost to lift it over the jumps!"

Yseulta clasped her hands together. Without her disfiguring gloves the Duke thought her long white fingers were very sensitive and almost as revealing as her eyes.

"It is wonderful to hear you speak like that of Papa," she said. "Everybody else only remembers..."

There was no need for her to say any more, and the Duke said,

"He made one mistake, but now you must forget it."

"How can I do that when Uncle Lionel keeps telling me that no one will ever want to speak to me or look at me except with ... loathing and disgust?"

She gave a little shiver as she spoke, then looked up at the Duke to ask,

"How can you have been so kind? Uncle Lionel was hoping you would shout and curse at me, as he would have done, and the carriage was waiting to drive me back with the servants laughing at my discomfiture."

The Duke's lips tightened. He loathed cruelty in whatever form he met it. He realised that the Marquess had meant him to torture this pathetic little creature, as he had obviously tortured her ever since her father's death. He took a sip of his brandy before he said,

"I have a proposition to put to you, and I think it is a very sensible one."

Yseulta looked at him apprehensively, and he said quickly,

"It is nothing frightening, but you may have to make rather an effort to do what I say."

"What is that?" Yseulta asked.

There was a tremor in her voice. He knew it had flashed through her mind that he intended to ask her to leave the train at the first stop. He did not know how he knew this, but he was sure that was what she was thinking, and he said,

"I said it was not frightening – in fact it is something you can make very enjoyable, if you do what I tell you."

He did not think she was really listening as he went on,

"Because you have been so unhappy about your father, and because you have been punished for his sins and not your own, I want you, while you are staying in Scotland as my guest, to forget the past completely and enjoy the present."

Yseulta stared at him. He thought she was wondering if he was speaking sincerely or was in some obscure way she did not comprehend, teasing her. She looked so very young and very helpless. At the same time she was so pathetic in her black gown, that he wanted to reassure her that he was completely sincere in what he was suggesting.

He had an idea however that if he explained that, it might make her more nervous than she was already. So he merely said quietly,

"Your uncle is a bully, and bullies always like to have something smaller and weaker than themselves whom they can terrorise. But now that you have escaped, forget him!"

"That is what I want to do," Yseulta murmured.

"I do not think your idea of running away the minute you reach Scotland is a good one," the Duke said. "You are too young and pretty not to get into trouble."

Again he was aware that Yseulta was afraid to trust what he said. He realised, because she had obviously never been paid any compliments, that she was wondering if he really meant it.

"What would please me most," he went on quickly, "is that you should enjoy the ball my mother is giving, and of course admire my castle, which I think is very beautiful."

"Mama used to tell me about Scottish castles," Yseulta said, "And I have been longing to see one."

"Well, now you shall," the Duke smiled, "And I shall be very disappointed if you do not find mine the most beautiful of all. And while you are staying with me, I shall be deeply upset if you do not enjoy yourself."

"You ... you really want me to stay?" Yseulta asked in a whisper. "I am afraid your friends will think me very strange."

"Why should they do that?" the Duke asked.

As Yseulta looked away from him he realised it had been a foolish answer, and he said,

"You must be sensible about your father. I know it is difficult, but people forget, and you have the whole of your life in front of you. Remember, however unfortunate a mistake somebody may make, we can none of us put back the clock."

He felt as if Yseulta relaxed a little. Then she said,

"You are so kind, and because I know what you are suggesting is very intelligent, I will try to obey you."

She gave a wistful little smile as she added,

"I know I shall look strange at your house party – but a scapegoat is not a very pretty animal!"

Once again the Duke felt his anger rise. Every word Yseulta spoke told him all too clearly of the way in which she had been treated. The Marquess had tortured her with his continual references to her father's fraud and his subsequent suicide.

"Forget it!" he said sharply. "Forget everything! Just feel as if you have been born anew, dressed like a pretty debutante starting off your life with a profusion of balls, receptions and parties to make it extremely enjoyable."

Yseulta laughed, and it was a very pretty sound.

"You are making it into a fairy story," she said, "And I can only hope that it will last, at least until midnight!"

"If I am your Fairy Godfather," the Duke answered, "I promise you it will!"

"I want to believe you," Yseulta said. "I can almost see the pumpkin change into a carriage ... and the mice into magnificent horses!"

Then, as if she suddenly remembered the next part of the story, she looked away from him. He knew she was thinking that in her threadbare black gown, she would indeed look like a 'Cinderella'.

"What I am going to do," the Duke said as he finished his brandy, "Is to ask my friend Anthony to change places with me because I want to talk to my mother."

He moved away as he spoke and Yseulta, looking after him, told herself it could not be true. How could any man be so kind and so understanding? She wondered what her uncle would say when the carriage returned home without her. He would learn from the footman that she had been cordially invited onto the train, and had not been denounced and turned away contemptuously, as he had planned.

'Perhaps,' she thought, 'He will order me to return at once.'

She knew if he did so, despite what the Duke had said, she would have to run away and hide. There must be relatives of her mother, who were Sinclair's, living somewhere near the castle, which she knew was in the Highlands.

She wondered if it would be possible to get in touch with them. None of them had come to her mother's funeral, although one or two had written to say how sorry they were to learn of her death. Because she had never met any of them, and she knew that during the years of her marriage her mother had lost touch with her family, she had not kept any of their letters.

She had not even been interested in knowing where they lived, except that it was Scotland, and Scotland was a big place. Then she told herself that if the necessity arose she was sure her mother would help her! She had felt her beside her as she was approaching the train. She was sure now that having helped her escape from her uncle, her mother would somehow save her from having to go back.

'Help me, help me, Mama,' she prayed.

She felt her mother must know how exciting it was for her to be on the Duke's private train. She was still saying a little prayer when the Duke's friend Anthony came to sit down beside her.

"I have been planning with the Duchess the different reels we will dance at the ball," he explained. "But I suppose you do not know any of them."

"On the contrary," Yseulta replied, "I can 'Strip the Willow', dance the 'Eightsom', and I hope, unless they have changed, I am quite proficient in several others."

Anthony who was a handsome man, the same age as the Duke, exclaimed,

"That is certainly unexpected! Are you telling me you are Scottish?"

"My mother was a Sinclair," Yseulta said, "But I have never been to Scotland before."

"Then may I, as a MacDonald, welcome you to your native land?" Anthony said. "And I shall look to you to help the other girls to learn the reels quickly."

"Oh, please – do not ask me to do that," Yseulta pleaded. "I am afraid I was boasting when I told you I could dance the reels. In fact I have only danced them at children's parties when Mama always liked to have them, and Papa and his friends used to join in."

"If you are Scottish, it will come naturally to you," Anthony smiled.

Because he made it sound like the Duke's Fairy Story, Yseulta smiled back at him.

*

Meanwhile the Duke was talking to his mother. He showed her first the note that the Marquess had written to him and the Duchess gave an exclamation of disgust.

"How dare he be so rude to you!" she said angrily. "I have always thought him to be a thoroughly unpleasant man. Although his wife has never said so,

I have often thought that Sophie was not as happy as she ought to be."

"He has certainly contrived to make that wretched girl unhappy," the Duke remarked.

"It was very clever and quick-witted of you to keep her with us," his mother replied, "Rather than send her back, which was what the Marquess obviously expected."

"He treats her as a scapegoat," the Duke said, "And makes her wear mourning, even though there is no reason for it."

The Duchess stared at him.

"I cannot believe that can be true!"

"'The evil that men do lives after them'," the Duke quoted.

"I have never heard anything so cruel!" the Duchess said indignantly.

"I have told her that she must try to enjoy herself as if she was a debutante while she is at the castle," the Duke said. "Which means, Mama, you will have to try and find her some clothes. She can hardly attend the ball or spend the weekend looking as she does now!"

"I am sure I can arrange something," the Duchess said, "And I can only apologise, my dear, for thinking for one moment that Lady Sarah might suit you as a wife. You could certainly not have tolerated the Marquess as your father-in-law."

"It would give me great pleasure to tell him exactly what I think of him," the Duke said, "Except that that would mean sinking to his level. What I suggest we do, Mama, is to make a great fuss of Yseulta. I have a feeling, and I am sure I am not mistaken, that that will annoy the Marquess more than anything else!"

"I see your reasoning," the Duchess replied. "In the meantime, dearest, you will have to concentrate on the other two girls. Have you spoken to Beryl Wood?"

"One thing is quite obvious," the Duke replied. "She does not want to speak to me!"

The Duchess looked at him in astonishment.

"Why should you say that?"

"She has been looking extremely sulky ever since she boarded the train," the Duke explained, "And when I tried to speak to her, she said she wanted to be left alone, settled herself on the other side of the carriage and shut her eyes!"

He saw that his mother was looking perturbed and said,

"Never mind, Mama, perhaps she will cheer up when we reach the castle, and meantime I must talk to Lady Deborah."

"The Earl would certainly be a pleasanter father-in-law than the Marquess!"

"Though doubtless a very expensive one," the Duke replied. "Perry told me when he saw the girl coming down the platform that Fernhurst is in deep water."

"You mean he is in debt?" the Duchess enquired.

"Up to his ears, so Perry says!"

The Duchess sighed.

"Everything seems to be going wrong," she said. "But we have Saturday, Sunday and Monday before you have to make some decision."

"I suppose there is no alternative?" the Duke asked hopefully.

"Only to go back and face George Wallington."

There was no need to say that was impossible.

The Duke realised that at just about this time George Wallington would have crossed the Channel and reached Dover. He thought Hermione was probably thinking the same thing, and perhaps crying hopelessly because he had left her, and she had to face her husband alone.

He thought angrily that if he had been an ordinary man with no commitments, he would have stopped the train and gone back to London. They could then have faced George Wallington together and told him he could do his damnedest. But he knew, that not only he and Hermione would suffer from such a chivalrous action, but so would his mother and the whole of the MacVegon clan. And he was well aware that the clan was the most important.

As their chieftain he had responsibilities that were difficult for the English to understand. To a Scottish clan their chieftain was their shepherd, their father and above all their guide. They looked on him as if he was their king, to direct them, to help them and to protect them.

How, in that position, could he leave them to the mercy of his uncle? He had always been a rather stupid man with no male heir to succeed after him. The Duke was well aware that in Scotland a daughter could inherit her father's title and position if he had no son. The title itself was not particularly important, but he could not remember any clan that had had a woman as its chieftain.

He told himself that regardless of his personal feelings he was obliged, because he had been born who he was, to do his duty, however painful, however much it cost him. Not in money, but in happiness.

As if he knew that his mother might have sensed what he was feeling, he put his hand over hers. Then without speaking he rose to see where Deborah was sitting. He moved Hugo away from her side so that he could talk to her.

CHAPTER FIVE

The journey to Scotland was made as comfortable as possible. The private train stopped in a siding early in the evening so that the passengers could sleep. It only started again soon after breakfast.

There was a new landscape to see the next morning, and Yseulta sat at the window enthralled. When they passed through Perthshire with its high mountains and its deep rivers, she thought that nothing could be more beautiful.

They had an excellent luncheon. When the afternoon was drawing to a close they drew into the small station, which she learnt had been built by the Duke's father. It was directly opposite the gates of the castle. Nevertheless there were carriages waiting to carry the guests down a long drive. At the far end of it was the castle itself with its high turrets and a tower on which was flying the Duke's standard.

Yseulta had had a glimpse of it already in the distance and saw that it was built above a bay of the sea. Being of pale grey stone it looked even more fairytale-like than she had expected it to be.

Now as she drove down the drive sitting beside Lady Beryl and Lady Deborah, with the Duke, Hugo and Anthony opposite them, the expression on her face was very revealing. It made the Duke say with a smile,

"Now tell me what you think of my castle."

"I am terrified that it will vanish before I can get inside!" Yseulta replied in a rapt voice.

The Duke laughed, but while Lady Deborah agreed that it was very attractive, Lady Beryl said nothing. She had hardly spoken all the time they were in the train. Yseulta had the idea that when the Duke came near her or spoke to her she almost shuddered. She was not aware of course that the Duchess had noticed something was wrong and had said to Janet, her lady's maid,

"I wonder what is wrong with Lady Beryl Wood. I do hope she is not sickening for some illness!"

She was not surprised when Janet had the answer.

"The trouble is, Your Grace, Lady Beryl didn't want to come to Scotland, and she's afraid she might be invited to stop here."

The Duchess looked surprised and Janet went on,

"I was talking to her lady's maid, and she tells me there was a real "Ow-d'ye-do' when 'Er Ladyship was told you'd invited her."

"But why?" the Duchess asked. "I do not understand."

"'Er Ladyship's in love, Your Grace, and was hoping to be married in the autumn."

"Good Heavens!" the Duchess exclaimed. "I never thought of that! In which case, why did she not refuse to come?"

"That's what 'Er Ladyship wanted to do, but her father were ever so delighted at the thought of her becoming a Duchess!"

There was silence for a moment. Then the Duchess said,

"You mean the Duke of Charnwood guessed that was why she was being asked?"

"Of course, Your Grace," Janet said. "They were saying in the servants' hall that the only way His Grace could avoid a scandal would be to go abroad or get married!"

The Duchess had long ago given up being surprised at what was known by the servants, often before it reached the dining room. Janet was an inveterate gossip, and the Duchess was well aware that the lady's maids of her friends all talked. There was little that went on in Mayfair that was not known to them.

She did not say any more, but she sighed as she thought that as far as marriage was concerned, it would now have to be Lady Deborah. She was pretty and, as she had thought originally, a suitable bride for Kenyon.

At the same time, because he was so fastidious and his love affairs had always been with sophisticated women, she was certain that Lady Deborah's habit of giggling at everything would soon irritate him.

'It was very foolish of me,' she told herself, 'not to have made enquiries as to whether Beryl's heart was engaged before I invited her to the Castle.'

Actually she had supposed that as Beryl, Deborah and Sarah were all debutantes, they would not have had time to lose their hearts and would therefore find the Duke irresistible. There was however nothing she could do now. She therefore arranged that the three girls, with the Duke and two of his friends, should arrive at the castle together.

The horses took them slowly down the drive, which was bordered on each side with fir trees. More fir trees stretched away on either side of the castle, but Yseulta could still see little glimpses of the sea. Behind them the moors rose sharply towards the sky making, she thought, a fitting background for the most beautiful castle she had ever imagined.

As they drove a little nearer there was the sound of the Duke's pipers standing outside the front door to welcome him home. It was the first time that Yseulta had ever heard the pipes.

While Deborah put her fingers in her ears and Beryl looked indifferent, she felt a strange excitement in her breast.

"The pipes!" she said in a whisper.

The Duke heard her and bent forward.

"They are playing a welcome to me as chieftain," he explained, "and I feel somewhat remiss that I have not changed into my kilt."

"It will be very exciting to see you in it!" Yseulta exclaimed.

The Duke realised that she was not paying him a flirtatious compliment such as he might have received from an older woman. She was genuinely thrilled as a child would have been by everything that was happening. It was all part of the fairy story he had created for her.

There were kilted servants waiting at the front door to usher them in. They ascended a broad staircase, where the walls were decorated with stag horns, into a large and beautiful drawing room. It was on the first floor and looked out over the bay.

Directly below the castle there was a garden bright with flowers enclosed by a wall beyond which was some rough land overlooking the waves of the North Sea. It was all so beautiful, including the room itself, that Yseulta was silent because there were no words in which to express her feelings.

As if the Duke understood, he told her quietly how long ago the castle had first been built as a fortress against the Danes. Later it had been enlarged by each succeeding chieftain. Then it had been burnt down at the end of the 18th century and only the tower was left of the original building.

"It was my grandfather who built it up as it is now," he finished, "and I would like to think that it is one of the finest castles in the whole of Scotland!"

"Nothing could be more magnificent!" Yseulta cried.

Then she was silent because she could still hear the pipers playing outside as they moved round the castle. It was the Duchess who showed the guests to their bedrooms, and she had put the girls next to each other. The last of their rooms adjoined a turret. Its outer wall was curved, and this was the one given to Yseulta.

"I think you will be comfortable here, my dear," the Duchess said. "Everybody loves this room because it has such a good view of the sea."

"Thank you, you are so very kind."

Then, as the Duchess would have left her, she asked,

"Please, may I say something to you?"

"Yes, of course, my dear. What is it?" the Duchess enquired.

"His Grace, and the gentleman who was arranging the reels, have talked about the ball, but I feel sure you will understand that it would be better if I did not take part in it."

She spoke hesitatingly and the Duchess looked at her in surprise before she said,

"I heard you know the reels, so of course we want you to dance them."

Yseulta looked shy. Then she said,

"But I should look very strange, because I have no proper evening gown, only a dress I bought when Mama died and it is now too small for me."

She spoke in an apologetic little voice and the Duchess realised how embarrassed she was at what she had to say. The Duchess shut the bedroom door. Then she said,

"Listen, Yseulta, my son has shown me the letter your uncle wrote to him, and I am surprised and shocked that any man, especially a relative, should treat you in such an appalling manner!"

She saw that Yseulta was listening and went on,

"Of course you must come to my ball and, although we have very little time, I am sure we can find a pretty gown for you to wear."

She saw Yseulta's expression change and went on,

"I will also find something more suitable than black for you to walk on the moors, and perhaps, as I intend to do, to watch the men catch salmon in the river."

As she finished speaking the tears came into Yseulta's eyes and she asked,

"Do you really mean that? I know I ought not to worry you. At the same time I am very aware of how terrible I look."

The Duchess smiled.

"Your face is very lovely, my dear, and that is something which cannot be spoilt."

Because she had known no kindness in the last two years, the tears overflowed and ran down Yseulta's cheeks.

"It is difficult to know how to thank you," she said in a stifled voice.

"Then do not try," the Duchess said, "just leave everything to me. I will go now and talk to my housekeeper and see what we can find you."

She walked out of the bedroom and found outside in the passage a footman was carrying Yseulta's basket-type luggage. A housemaid followed who was to unpack it. The Duchess walked towards her own room, but before she reached it, she met the Duke.

"Oh, there you are, Mama!" he said. "I was just coming to tell you that tea is ready in the Robert the Bruce Room."

"I am just coming," the Duchess said, "but first I must speak to Mrs. Ross."

Mrs. Ross was the housekeeper, and the Duke was just about to say that Mrs. Ross could wait when the Duchess went on,

"I have to find that poor child something decent to wear. Can you imagine anything crueller than refusing to buy her anything new for two years so that she has grown out of everything she possesses?"

"I would like to tell the Marquess what I think of him," the Duke said angrily.

"So would I," the Duchess answered. "At the same time, I think the mere fact that you did not turn Yseulta away as he expected will give him something to think about!"

The Duchess did not wait for her son to reply and hurried towards her own bedroom. As she expected, Mrs. Ross, who had been housekeeper at the castle for nearly forty years, was looking to see that everything was in order.

"How are you, Mrs. Ross?" the Duchess asked, holding out her hand.

"The better for seeing Your Grace," Mrs. Ross replied with a curtsey.

"Now, what I want," the Duchess said, "Is for you to find some clothes for Miss Yseulta Corde. She has nothing she can possibly wear, and I feel certain you have some things of mine that would fit her."

Mrs. Ross looked surprised but the Duchess went on,

"She is very thin, so they can be taken in. What is more important than anything else is that she needs a pretty gown to wear at the ball."

She thought as she spoke that that was going to be difficult because as a young girl Yseulta should wear white. Her own gowns were all of deeper colours or of the soft pigeon's grey that looked so beautiful on Princess Alexandra.

"You leave it to me, Your Grace," Mrs. Ross said in a tone of satisfaction. "I've got Your Grace's tartan skirts that you discarded when you first came to the castle thirty-five years ago, and there are some pretty gowns that I've kept just in case one day they would come in useful."

The Duchess laughed.

"I might have known, Mrs. Ross, that you would have the answer to any problem! Now, as His Grace wants me to pour out the tea, will you go and talk to Miss Corde?"

She paused to say finally,

"Throw away those horrible black garments she has been wearing for the last two years. They are only fit for the dustbin!"

*

It seemed to Yseulta as if Mrs, Ross waved a magic wand that was in keeping with everything else in the castle. She missed her tea in the Robert the Bruce Room, but a tray was brought to her in her bedroom.

As she ate the girdle cakes, Mrs. Ross, assisted by two housemaids, carried in a profusion of skirts, blouses, and coats from some hidden 'Aladdin's Cave' at the top of the castle. Some of the gowns took Yseulta's breath away. As Mrs. Ross had told the Duchess, she had hoarded everything year by year that her mistress discarded.

The gowns that the Duchess had brought to the castle when she married the Third Duke were still looking lovely. They had been made by one of the most expensive dressmakers in London and the materials were ageless.

Not only had the Duchess's family, who were very rich, expended large sums on her as a girl, but the Duke, who was madly in love with his beautiful wife, had also taken her to Paris. He bought her the fantastic creations of Frederick Worth, whose designs were unrivalled in the ensuing years.

There were two seamstresses working in the castle, who were quite capable of turning a crinoline or a heavily bustled gown into something more fashionable. It was so much easier, they said, to take away material than to put it in.

As Yseulta tried on first one gown, then another, they showed her how, by removing an enormous bustle or a crinoline they could create something up to date. In fact, exactly what the other young ladies in the party would be wearing.

They certainly worked very quickly, although the gown in which Yseulta entered the drawing room that evening was only tacked together and she had been sewn into it. Nevertheless, when she looked at herself in the mirror she could hardly believe it was true.

Of very pale blue, the gown showed the soft curves of her figure. The skirt was swept to the back to form a very small bustle, which was now in fashion. The seamstresses had arranged the décolletage of the bodice so that it just went over her shoulders. She had been afraid that it might be too revealing, but in fact the gown was simpler than those the other girls were wearing. However it showed off her long neck, while the colour accentuated the strange paleness of her hair.

In fact the Duke thought, as she came into the drawing room where they were to meet before dinner, that her hair was exactly the colour of the first fingers of the dawn. Then he was aware of the reason why he had seen so many dawns recently and with an effort deliberately put the thought of Hermione aside.

He had thought somewhat wistfully last night as he went to bed on the train that it would be best if he never saw her again, at least not for a long time. He was quite certain that if they met she would look at him in that revealing manner which, to say the least of it, was very indiscreet. When he did return to London, everybody would be watching for any intimacies between them if they appeared together in public.

'I shall have to stay in Scotland,' he thought.

It was scarcely a hardship at the moment with the fishing at its best, and in a month or so there would be the grouse. After that, when the guests had left, he wondered if he would find life at the castle intolerable. At the same time, he told himself that if he had to stay in Scotland, unless he went abroad, he would miss his estate in the country and his horses running at Newmarket.

The whole thing was intolerable! Whatever George Wallington might do, he would go back and 'Face the music'. Then he told himself that worse than anything else, he would not only have himself to think about in the future, but also a wife.

He had a sudden vision in the darkness of Beryl Wood's sulky face, and he thought he could hear Deborah Hurst giggling. Then he could see Hermione's lips raised to his and feel the softness of her body close to his.

'How can I bear it?' he asked himself.

There was no answer. He knew as the train started up the next morning that the wheels were carrying him further and further away from the one thing he found really enjoyable.

*

There was no doubt that the house party was surprised at Yseulta's appearance. They had thought she looked strange when she joined the train at King's Cross. Yet they had not liked to ask questions in case she had recently been bereaved. For her part the Duchess had no wish for her friends to know how abominably the Marquess had insulted her son.

Now as Yseulta came into the drawing room, nervous and feeling self-conscious, there was a sudden silence. Then Perry, who like the Duke was wearing a kilt, exclaimed,

"You look as though you have just stepped down from the sky!"

Yseulta laughed, and it broke the tension.

"Actually," she said, "I feel as if I might have been carried up into it, and perhaps we are no longer on Earth, but visiting Mars!"

"Now you are being modest," one of the older guests joined in, "and if we are on some other planet, looking as you do, it must be Venus!"

Everybody laughed at that, and a footman offered Yseulta a glass of champagne, which she refused. The

Duke, however, lifted one off the tray and put it into her hand.

"As this is your first visit to Scotland," he said, "I think you must celebrate it by drinking a toast to a country whose blood runs in your veins."

"I would like to do that," Yseulta said.

The Duke raised his glass.

"To Scotland!" he said. "And may you always be proud to be a Scot!"

"I am very, very proud," Yseulta replied, "and also very excited!"

There was no doubt about that, the Duke thought, as he noticed her looking round the huge dining hall. The portraits of previous Dukes hung on the wall interspersed between the stags' heads and antlers.

Then, as was customary towards the end of the meal, his piper came into the dining hall playing the pipes and walking round the table. As he did so, the Duke watched Yseulta. He thought the stars in her eyes and the way she clasped her fingers together with delight as she watched the piper, was very moving.

In contrast, Deborah once again had her fingers in her ears, and he heard Beryl say quite audibly above the sound of the pipes,

"I loathe the bagpipes! I think, without exception, they make the most uncivilised music I have ever heard!"

When dinner was over the older members of the party settled down once again to play bridge. It was suggested that the young people might enjoy card games that involved them all. The Duchess thought there was rather a cynical twist to her son's mouth, but he did not refuse to join in. His friends suggested a rowdy game called 'Racing Demon' and made side-bets between themselves. Even Lady Beryl became quite excited over this.

There was no doubt that Yseulta, once she understood what she had to do, thought more quickly, and moved more quickly than any of the others. She was the winner. When the gentlemen applauded her she said modestly that she had just been lucky. When one of the players rose to have a drink she moved automatically to the window where she opened the curtain to look out into the darkness…

The stars filled the sky, and there was a young moon, which was just beginning to throw its light on the sea. She felt as though the sheer loveliness of it seemed to fill her heart.

For the first time in what seemed years she felt happy. It was not only because her uncle was not there to shout at her or strike her. It was because the beauty she saw was flooding into her heart. It was as if her mother's arms were round her and she was safe, and there was nothing to make her tremble or want to cry.

"I thought you would find this beautiful," a deep voice said beside her.

It was the Duke, but she did not turn her head to look at him.

"I was just thinking," she said, "that it has made me so happy that I cannot believe I am still alive on Earth!"

The Duke did not answer for a moment. Then he said,

"I suppose we are all looking for happiness, but it means different things to different people."

"Of course," Yseulta agreed, "and I think the happiness we all seek is something so spiritual that it cannot be hurt or spoilt by human beings."

The Duke knew she was saying what she was feeling, and after a moment he answered,

"You are quite right, and perhaps we make what we call happiness too personal, too dependent on others, rather than on ourselves."

Yseulta smiled.

"That is what I was thinking," she said, "and nothing can ever take this from me."

She made a gesture towards the sea, the sky, the stars and the moon, and the Duke knew exactly what she was trying to say. At the same time, as if he felt he must think it out for himself he said,

"But that can also make one feel lonely."

"That is true," Yseulta agreed, "and that was why Papa could not bear life any longer when Mama … died."

It was the first time she had talked about her father and mother for a long time. Yet the words seemed to come quite naturally from her lips.

"So they loved each other very much," the Duke said softly.

"They were part of one another and, when Mama left Papa, he lost half of himself."

Yseulta's voice was very moving. Then as if she was suddenly aware that she was talking very intimately to a stranger, she gave him an apologetic little smile as she asked,

"Do you want me to go back to the table?"

"There is no hurry," the Duke said, "and one evening when everybody is not tired, I will take you up onto the tower where my ancestors' private guards kept watch for the invaders approaching in their great ships."

"The Vikings!"

"The Vikings," the Duke agreed, "and I think that is why you and I have fair hair in a country where the people are predominantly dark or red-headed."

Yseulta laughed.

"I have never thought of that before, but of course it is a very romantic idea, and I expect lots of people have told you that you look like a Viking."

The Duke thought that the women who had loved him, more often compared him to a Greek God. Most of them knew so little about Scotsmen that they had no idea of the Viking raids to which at one time the people were very vulnerable. The Duke was about to tell her there was what he had always believed to be a Viking ship buried amongst the fir trees near the beach, when they were interrupted by Hugo.

"Deborah wants to have another game before we go to bed," he said. "Do come and join us."

"Yes, of course," the Duke agreed.

He turned away, but Yseulta took one last look at the beauty outside before she too joined the others.

'It is mine,' she thought, 'And whatever happens in the future no one can take that away from me!'

*

The following day was Sunday and Yseulta learned, when she was called, that the Duchess would be going to the kirk. She had said that if her guests were too tired they should take the opportunity to rest.

"I would like to go to the kirk," Yseulta said.

Mrs. Ross cleverly provided her with a very pretty gown that had a wide scarf to wear with it if it was cold. She saw to her delight that there was a chip-straw bonnet trimmed with flowers and pale green ribbons to go with it.

There was however breakfast first, in a different room from where they had had tea, and which was filled with morning sunshine. As Yseulta entered, there was only the Duchess sitting at the table with the Duke beside her. They both looked up in surprise as Yseulta came in.

"You are early, my dear," the Duchess said. "I suggested that if anyone was tired, they should have breakfast in their rooms and rise later."

"I am not in the least tired," Yseulta replied, "and if I will not be a nuisance, I would love to come to the kirk with you."

"But of course we shall be very pleased to have you!" the Duchess replied. "But you may find the service a little different from what you are used to at home."

There was a little pause before Yseulta said,

"I-I have not been allowed to go to church since I came to live with Uncle Lionel."

"Why ever not?" the Duke asked without thinking.

Then he remembered what the Marquess thought of Yseulta and therefore would not allow her to appear in public. Because he realised he had made a mistake, he rose to the side-table to help her from the silver dishes from which the guests helped themselves as was customary in big houses.

As he sat down again Yseulta saw he was eating porridge out of a wooden bowl with a silver rim. She looked at it with interest.

"I remember Mama telling me that Scotsmen always eat their porridge standing," she said after a moment. The Duke laughed.

"That was when we were afraid that some opposing clansmen would attack us unawares," he replied. "But I think, at the moment, I am safe in my own castle!"

"I hope so," Yseulta said. "It would be unfortunate if the McGregors, the Macdonalds or the McKenzies besieged you."

"I feel safe enough," the Duke replied. "And anyway, I have you and Mama to protect me!"

"Stop talking nonsense," the Duchess said, "or we shall be late for the kirk! And do not forget that the Minister will expect you to read the lesson."

I can only hope," the Duke answered, "that in celebration of my presence he does not preach interminably!"

The Duchess smiled.

"You warned him last time, so I think we can expect a sermon that will not last for more than half-an-hour!"

She was teasing her son, but he groaned before he said,

"I warn you, if that is the case, I shall fall asleep."

They went downstairs to where the carriage was waiting. Yseulta thought that no one could look more impressive than the Duke in his kilt and day sporran, which had the head of a badger. Last night when he had a jabot at this throat and a chieftain's sporran with a silver top, she had thought no man could look more magnificent.

The kirk was not large and was very cold. The Minister in his black robes met the Duke at the door and escorted him to the family pew. When they were seated Yseulta looked at the congregation.

They were very interesting and she felt sure that most of them were of the MacVegon clan. There were old men with long beards and stalwart young ones who she was certain were guides and gillies. At the very back of the kirk there were men with their dogs at their feet, and she guessed they were shepherds. There were small children who also wore kilts made of the Duke's tartan.

The congregation sang with gusto the hymns, which they knew so well that there was no need to refer to the hymn book.

Yseulta had the idea anyway that most of them were unable to read.

The sermon she found very interesting because the minister spoke of the Highland Clearances as if they had happened yesterday, rather than having ended at least fifty years earlier.

When the service was over the Duke was the first to leave the kirk. Then as everybody followed him the elders came up to speak to him respectfully. He talked to them about the prospects of the grouse and enquired how good the lambing had been.

As they went back to the Castle, the Duchess said,

"It is obvious that everybody turned out to see you, dearest. Two Sundays ago, when I went to the kirk alone, there were not half so many people present."

"Then it is a good thing I did not oversleep," the Duke remarked with a twinkle in his eyes.

As they drove back to the castle, Yseulta was looking up at the moors and she asked,

"Would it be all right for me to walk up the hill? I would not want to disturb the birds in any way."

"You will not disturb them," the Duke replied, "and as it is something I would like to do myself, I will take you to the cascade, which is my favourite walk."

"I would love that!" Yseulta exclaimed.

"I expect the others would also like to go with you," the Duchess said, "especially Deborah, who has never been to Scotland before."

Yseulta wished for a moment that she could go alone with the Duke, then thought it presumptuous of her. Of course he would want to be accompanied by all the others. At the same time, she knew that with Deborah's giggling and Hugo and Perry making everybody laugh with their jokes, she would not feel the beauty of it, as she had last night.

She had a feeling that the silence of the moors, except for the birds, would be very moving. She wanted, too, to see the cascade falling down the side of the hill and running over the stones towards the sea.

As the carriage turned down the drive, she saw the castle at the end of it and knew there was so much to explore. So much else to see in this 'Wonderland' in which she found herself. Every minute was a new experience but, at the same time, something that she might never have again.

'Oh please God,' she prayed, 'do not let the time go too quickly.'

She had the terrifying feeling that she was being swept along by a fast current. Almost before she could catch her breath, she would have to make a momentous decision. Whether she would return to England and her uncle or run away into the unknown.

CHAPTER SIX

Walking up the twisting sheep path towards the moors, Yseulta felt a thrill of excitement, which she knew was because she was Scottish. Her mother had talked to her so often of the beauty of the moors, the purple of the heather, and the lights that she had said could only be found in Scotland. Now she was seeing them for herself, and she knew that nothing could be more thrilling.

After luncheon, at which everyone had been amusing and witty, the Duchess said she was going to rest, adding that everybody else could do as they liked.

"Remember, it is the Sabbath in Scotland, and the elders of our clan are very strict about us behaving with propriety."

She was smiling as she spoke. At the same time, Yseulta knew that she was giving them all a warning. Her mother had told her how strict the Scottish were about Sunday. She had realised when she watched the people in the Kirk how devout they all were. She knew what she wanted to do, and to her joy no one except the Duke wished to go for a walk.

Lady Beryl said quickly that she had some letters to write, and it was quite obvious to the Duchess to whom she would be writing.

Lady Deborah looked meaningfully at Hugo who said,

"I promised I would take you out in a boat, and as the sea is calm today, I do not think you will be seasick."

"I am never sick at sea!" Lady Deborah replied indignantly, then realised that once again he was teasing her.

Finally when the older guests had said they were going to sit in the garden in the sunshine, Yseulta and the Duke set off alone. They were not aware as they walked up the drive that the Duchess was watching them with a worried expression in her eyes. Only a few minutes after they had passed through the great gates they reached the moorland. Then they were climbing, and there was nothing to break the silence save the warning *'Caw'* of a cock grouse as it soared at their approach, winging its way along the side of the hill. Only when they had climbed for quite a long way did the Duke say,

"Now – turn around!"

Yseulta did so, and she saw beneath them the turrets and towers of the Castle. There was the garden beneath it and the blue of the sea stretching away into a misty horizon. It was so beautiful, so exactly what she had hoped to see. She sat down on the heather and just felt her own being merge into the beauty of it. She forgot the Duke was there, and had no idea that he was watching her, until he said quietly,

"Now tell me what you are thinking."

"It is just as I imagined it would be," Yseulta said, "only a million times more marvellous!"

He smiled.

"That is what I always feel when I come home."

"How can you ever bear to go away?" she asked.

There was a pause before he replied,

"I also enjoy being at my house in Oxfordshire, and of course, seeing my horses on the racecourse."

"I can understand that," Yseulta said, "but you also spend a lot of time in London."

The Duke thought he could not tell her the reason for this, and instead he replied,

"I have certain duties at Court, and it is a mistake to let the Sassenachs forget Scotland! We must remind them that we have a lot to offer them, if only they will bother to look for it."

Yseulta turned her face towards him.

"You are right! Of course, you are right!" she cried. "Mama always said that the English did not understand how much Scotland had to give to the world."

"It is interesting you should say that," the Duke answered, "because it is something I have always thought myself. But I am not certain what I can do about it."

"I am sure, if you wanted to, you could do a great deal," Yseulta answered, "and because you are who you are, the English would listen to you."

"Now you are not only inspiring me, but also offering me a challenge!" he said.

He spoke lightly, but Yseulta said in a wistful little voice,

"That is what I would like to do. Because Scotland is so beautiful it must never be ignored or forgotten."

After a little while they walked on. Now below them in a valley Yseulta could see the winding river in which the Duke told her he and his friends caught salmon.

"Can I come and watch you tomorrow?" Yseulta asked.

Then she thought perhaps she was pushing herself forward and added quickly,

"But only if I should be no trouble."

"I would like you to come," he said, "and perhaps you would like to fish yourself?"

"Could I do that?"

"It is not very difficult, and I am sure you will have 'beginner's luck' and catch your first salmon."

To his surprise Yseulta did not speak for a moment. Then she said in a very low voice,

"How is it possible that anyone can be so kind to me as you have been? I shall never, never forget it."

"I told you to enjoy yourself," the Duke said, "and now forget the past. There is always the future."

He knew even as he spoke that the future for Yseulta was bleak and very frightening. He was aware she had two choices of action. She could return to her uncle to be abused and tormented as she had been before, or find somewhere she could hide, without money or friends.

He decided it was something he would discuss with his mother. Perhaps they could find her a position of some sort where she could earn a little money and at the same time be safe. The Duke was well aware however that, looking as she did, it would be hard to find Yseulta employment. No woman would want to engage anyone so lovely if she had a husband and grown sons. It would also be quite impossible for her to live alone without some sort of chaperon who could protect her from men – who would find her irresistible.

'I will have to do something about her,' the Duke told himself.

Yet for the moment he could not think what it could be.

They walked on and were now moving downhill towards the sea. Because the Duke thought it a good idea to change the subject he said,

"Not far from here is a Pictish fort where I used to play when I was a boy. In fact I actually dug a great deal out from the grass and earth that had accumulated on top of it over the centuries."

"I would love to see it!" Yseulta said. "It sounds very exciting!"

"I used to think so," the Duke said, "and I believed the sightseers like yourself would enjoy visiting it."

"Oh, let us do that," she pleaded.

They walked on, and now there was not so much heather and the ground was very rough. Then suddenly, from behind a tussock, a man sprang up and came towards them. He had a wild look about him. His garments were in rags, while his feet were protruding through the holes in his shoes.

He ran towards them. When he reached them he pulled an evil-looking dirk out from his waist and shouted at the Duke something that he could not understand.

Then as the man raised his dirk the Duke flung his arm across Yseulta to protect her. But to his astonishment she stepped between him and the man with the dirk and, speaking the same language that he had, asked him a question. Whatever it was she said, it stayed his hand, and although his arm was still raised, he was for the moment still.

"What is it? What does he want?" the Duke asked sharply.

Yseulta answered him.

"He says he is starving," she explained, "and unless we give some money, his wife and children will die."

The Duke realised somewhat belatedly that the man had spoken Gaelic, and Yseulta had replied in the same tongue.

"Starving?" he exclaimed. "Ask him who he is."

In a gentle voice Yseulta asked the question, and the man, as he replied, slowly lowered his hand holding the dirk. He mumbled some words and the Duke realised he had said his name was "MacVegon".

"If he is a member of my clan," he said, "why is he starving, and where is he living?"

Yseulta translated what the Duke had said, only pausing when she was not sure of the Gaelic word. Then the man answered her. Now he spoke passionately, holding out his hands to demonstrate what he was saying. He looked first at Yseulta, then at the Duke as if he would compel them to understand his predicament. Finally he paused for breath and Yseulta explained,

"He has come a long way with his wife and two children because the croft where they were living tumbled down and was no longer habitable. He asked the help of somebody in the village."

As she spoke she pointed to where the river ended and went on,

"I think it was your factor, but he said he could do nothing for them, and so they have been sleeping in your Pictish fort."

She paused for a moment. Then she added a little shyly,

"His wife is going to have a baby and he is frightened that it will be born out here on the moor with no help."

She locked up pleadingly at the Duke and he replied, as she was willing him to do,

"We must of course do something for them. Tell him to take us to his wife and children."

He thought as he spoke that the smile that illuminated Yseulta's face was very lovely. The man went ahead of them, leaping over the heather so that his kilt, which was nothing but a piece of ragged cloth, flew out as he went downhill.

When they reached the Pictish fort, Yseulta could see that they had fastened a piece of tarpaulin over one corner of it. Under it were sitting a woman very large with child, and two small boys. The children were as ragged as their father, and they were very thin. They sat listlessly on the ground, only looking rather frightened when Yseulta and the Duke appeared. The woman too was obviously frightened and would have risen to her feet, but Yseulta stopped her.

"Do not try to get up," she said in Gaelic.

"Oi be awfu' tired," the woman murmured in English.

"It is hardly surprising when you have come such a long way," Yseulta replied, "and your husband says you are all hungry."

"Verry hungry," the woman replied. "We bring taties wi' us, but they all finished."

Yseulta looked at the Duke.

"You must come to the castle," he said, "and I will find you somewhere to stay at least until your baby arrives. When is it due?"

For a moment the woman looked puzzled. Then as if she understood she said,

"Now – verry soon!"

The Duke turned to Yseulta.

"Tell the man," he said, "that if he is a member of my clan I will look after them."

Yseulta said it first in Gaelic. Then as the woman understood and gave a little cry of joy, she saw the man go down on one knee and kiss the Duke's hand. It was the age-old gesture of allegiance to a chieftain.

She thought it very moving. Then she heard the Duke say to the woman,

"Now follow me as quickly as you can. I must see you are comfortable before nightfall."

Yseulta felt the tears come into her eyes at the expression of gratitude on the woman's face. She knew how frightening it must have been to think she would have to give birth on the moors with only her husband to help her. The little boys jumped to their feet as Yseulta and the Duke started to move down the hill towards the castle. Only when the path widened and they could walk side by side did Yseulta say,

"Those poor people! They must have walked for miles! The children's legs were scratched and bleeding from the heather."

"I am extremely annoyed with my factor!" the Duke said sharply. "He should have found them some place to go, or he could have appealed to the elders."

There was silence for a moment. Then Yseulta said,

"You may think it presumptions of me, but I am sure from what I have read that the factors in Scotland, when their masters are away, have often been cruel and indifferent to the clansmen."

"In other words you are blaming me!" the Duke exclaimed.

"Of course, you would never let anything happen like that knowingly," Yseulta said quickly, "but a factor is only a paid servant, and these are your people."

She paused then added hesitatingly,

"They belong to you and it is for the chieftain of the clan to help those in distress."

She thought when she had spoken that she had said too much. But she had in fact heard of the cruelties of the Clearances from her mother. How it was the factors in their Masters' absence who had let the people starve or burnt their cottages over their heads so as to leave the ground free for the sheep. Then, as she could not bear the Duke to be angry with her, she said in a frightened little voice,

"Please ... forgive me. I should not have said that to you when I know how very kind you are."

"No, no, you are quite right!" the Duke replied. "I have been away for too long. I shall send for my factor tomorrow and find out exactly what is happening on my land, and how many of my clan are without work and without homes."

"That will be a wonderful thing to do."

As she spoke she looked up at him admiringly, and for a moment he seemed about to say something, then changed his mind. They only had a little further to go before they reached the castle. There, as if he was waiting for his master, on the steps was the Duke's special servant Douglas, resplendent in his kilt and plaid. The Duke told Douglas what had happened and asked him where they could put the people who had been in the Pictish fort.

"They must have a roof over their heads tonight," he said, "and tomorrow I will make enquiries as to whether there is an empty croft. Then I must find some work for the man."

"I thinks, Yer Grace, the best thing for 'em ternight," Douglas replied, "would be the rooms at the back o' the stable which we keep for visitin' coachmen."

"Of course! That will be excellent!" the Duke said. "I'll get somebody to show them the way as soon as they arrive. Meanwhile I want you to go and order food for them from the kitchen – anything that is ready, and milk for the children."

As Douglas turned away to obey, the Duke realised that Yseulta was looking at him with starry eyes.

"This is another fairy tale," she said softly.

He smiled at her and said,

"Now, let us go and look at their accommodation."

They walked to the stables, which were at the back of the castle, and the Head Groom came hurrying at the Duke's appearance. He told him what he wanted, and they were shown two rooms at the back of the harness room. There was a kitchen with a small table, several hard chairs and a small coal-stove.

"Get the stove going," the Duke ordered.

"Aye, Yer Grace, Ah'll do tha'," the Head Groom replied.

It was then Yseulta saw that in the next room there was a large bed with a pile of horse blankets put tidily in one corner.

"The small boys can sleep on those," she said.

"Yes, of course," the Duke agreed, "and they will also acquire blankets."

"They'll be in the cupboard, Yer Grace," the Head Groom said.

He opened a cupboard as he spoke and Yseulta saw there was quite a number of thick lambs' wool blankets. It made her feel happy to know that neither the children, nor their mother would be cold or hungry tonight. Then because she felt a little shy at suggesting it, she said to the Duke in a low voice,

"I feel sure there must be a midwife in the village who should be told of the woman's condition."

"Yes, of course, you are right," the Duke agreed.

He gave the order, then as they walked back into the yard the family from the Pictish fort appeared. Yseulta had the idea that they had walked very quickly, afraid the Duke might change his mind or forget about them.

The woman was looking flushed. The man was carrying the smaller boy as if he was too tired and too exhausted from lack of food to be able to walk. The

Duke led them into the rooms he had arranged for them.

As he did so, Douglas appeared with two other men, carrying trays of food, which they set down on the table. The small boys seized a loaf of bread and pulling it apart started to thrust it into their mouths. Their mother would have remonstrated with them, but Yseulta said,

"Sit down and rest. You must be very tired, and His Grace has asked for a midwife to come to you as soon as possible."

Two tears rolled down the woman's cheeks. As she tried to wipe them away with the back of her dirty hand Yseulta walked to the Duke's side and said,

"I think we should leave them. They are all right now, and they are too emotional to express their feelings."

The Duke, who had been watching the small boys ravenously devouring anything they could get their hands on, smiled at her.

"You are right," he said, "and we can come and see them tomorrow."

The man tried to stammer his thanks in Gaelic, but the Duke and Yseulta moved away. As they walked back to the front door of the castle, Yseulta said almost as if she spoke to herself,

"This time the pumpkin has turned into a comfortable shelter with a feast fit for a king!"

The Duke laughed.

She felt as they walked up the steps and in through the front door that he did not wish to speak of his kindness. He was instead thinking that nobody on his land should be so near to starvation, or as desperate as the man had been when he had threatened them with his dirk. They had tea. Then as the Duchess and the elderly lady guests said they were going to rest before dinner, Yseulta had a sudden idea.

She was so afraid that her visit to the castle would come to an end before she had had time to see all of it. She therefore slipped out of the drawing room and went first to the Chieftain's Room, which she knew was being prepared for the ball.

It was the room where the chieftain of the MacVegon clan received the elders and his clansmen. The walls were covered with antlers and there was the huge heraldic coat-of-arms of the MacVegons at one end. At the other end of the room there was an arrangement of swords and battle-axes, shields and dirks that had been collected for generations.

The setting sun was coming through a long window and the sky was turning to crimson and gold. Yseulta suddenly thought how beautiful it would look from the top of the tower. The Duke had promised to take her there, but she was sure he had forgotten. She therefore walked quickly along the passages to the door at the far end of the castle. She found it almost by instinct and was not surprised to find that the tower itself must have had very few changes since it was first built.

There was a heavy brass-studded oak door, which was open. Inside, by the light coming through the arrow-slits, she could see the twisting steps leading up to the top of the tower. She climbed quickly, eager to see the sunset, knowing it would be something she would never forget.

She reached the top, and the crenelated battlements were exactly as she expected them to be. As she stepped out through a narrow door she drew in her breath at the beauty of the light from the sinking sun reflected in the sea. In the great arc of the heavens overhead there was just the faintest touch of darkness. The lights on the moors stretching out towards the north were exquisite. She could see in the distance the fishing village and the mouth of the river.

Into the harbour were coming the last of the fishing boats, their sails billowing out in the wind. It was so beautiful, and so exactly what she had prayed she might see that somehow it was not a surprise when a deep voice said,

"I thought I would find you here!"

She did not look round. She merely felt her heart turn over in a strange way because the Duke was beside her. It was as if the light of the setting sun was burning in her breast. He came close to her and after a moment he said,

"I have stood here a hundred times, yet it always thrills me as if I have never seen it before."

"That is because," Yseulta said, "the beauty of it is too overwhelming to become completely ours when we first look at it. We need to look and look, and each time it gives us something new."

"That is what I feel," the Duke said, "and it awakens new ideas in my mind."

"Of course," Yseulta murmured, "but I have never seen anything as lovely as this!"

"Nor have I," the Duke agreed, but now he was looking at her.

He was thinking that nothing could be more beautiful than the sun on her hair, or the light in her huge eyes.

He looked at her for a long moment. Then he said very quietly,

"Yseulta – will you marry me?"

For a moment she did not move.

Then slowly, as if in a dream, she turned her face to look up at him.

"W-what did you say?" she asked in a whisper.

"I asked you to marry me," the Duke said. "I know now that you are everything I want in my wife – everything I thought I could never find."

Yseulta just stared at him. Then it seemed as if her face was transformed into something so dazzlingly beautiful that he knew he had never seen a woman look so lovely before. Instinctively his arms went round her and her body melted into his.

Then as he held her close and still closer, his lips found hers. To Yseulta it was as if the whole world had been lit by a dazzling light and she could not think. She could only feel an ecstasy and a wonder that was beyond anything she had dreamt of or imagined.

The Duke kissed her and went on kissing her until they were no longer on top of the castle. They were flying in the sky and were part of the glory of it so that they were no longer human, but Divine. Then as the Duke raised his head there was the sudden skirl of the bagpipes in the distance as the Pipers paraded round the castle at the going down of the sun.

It was then that Yseulta came back to reality. Slowly, her eyes on the Duke, she moved against the strength of his arms.

"I love you," she said very softly. "But you know what you have suggested is impossible – completely and absolutely impossible!"

Then, before he could stop her, she moved away from him, and slipped through the open door behind them. He heard her footsteps going down the stone steps. As they died away there was only the sound of the bagpipes. The Duke stared across the water with unseeing eyes into the darkening horizon.

*

Yseulta reached the bottom of the tower and ran as swiftly as she could to her bedroom. She reached it and shut the door to throw herself down on her bed and hide her face against the pillow.

Could it be true? Was it possible that the Duke had asked her to marry him? Then she knew it was the traditional end to a fairy story, but a fairy story that could never come true. If he loved her, she knew that she loved him with her whole heart, and that it would be impossible for her ever to love anyone in the same way again. At the same time, she was well aware of who she was.

For the Duke of Strathvegon, of all people, to contemplate marriage with her father's daughter was unthinkable. It was as impossible as telling the tides to cease moving, or the stars to fall from the sky.

A pariah dog, her uncle had often called her, a scapegoat, a thing of shame from whom any decent person would shrink in horror. How could any man make her his wife, let alone the Duke of Strathvegon?

'I must go away,' she told herself.

She thought that the sooner she did so, the better. How could she bear to see him and know that he was obliged to marry one of the party?

Both Lady Beryl and Lady Deborah were more than suitable. Then she told herself she must be mistaken. He could not really have said that he loved her. Every instinct in her body, every particle of her mind knew that when he had kissed her, they were complete – one person.

A man and a woman who were the other half of each other, as their Creator had intended.

'I love him and I cannot hurt him,' Yseulta said to herself. 'I must just be thankful, very, very thankful, to have known just once such wonder and ecstasy ... even though I cannot keep it.'

It was then the tears filled her eyes, but she would not let them fall. Deliberately she got off the bed and walking to the window looked out. Now the sun had gone, the stars were coming out and the garden below was in darkness.

'That is what my life will be in the future,' she thought miserably, 'But I will not complain. I will be grateful – deeply grateful to have been loved by anyone so wonderful, and that I was here in his Castle and he held me in his arms.'

She looked out into the darkness and said,

'Thank You, God, for letting me find love, but I know I must not hurt anyone so magnificent. Help me to go away without making a fuss and hide me somewhere where I will be safe.'

It was a wistful little prayer. She had the feeling she was already moving out of the castle along an endless, empty road that led nowhere. Then because she could not help it, she felt her heart leap because he had kissed her and because she would see him again.

'I will go away after the ball,' she told herself. 'There will be so much commotion going on that no one will notice when I leave, and by the morning I will be far away.'

She knew it was not going to be easy. But if the worst came to the worst, she would rather die than go back to her uncle.

'At least,' she told herself, 'If I die of starvation in the Pictish fort, I shall not have to listen to the abuse of Papa or the insults that Uncle Lionel is always throwing at me.'

But although she was trying to be brave, she knew that her heart was saying one thing, and one thing only.

'I love him! I love him! *I love him!*'

She could hear it repeated over and over again. She knew it was something she would hear for the rest of her life, wherever she might die.

*

When he left the tower the Duke felt as if he too had suddenly stepped into a dream.

He walked towards his study where he might be alone. He knew as he did so that what he had felt when he kissed Yseulta was very different from anything he had experienced before. Before in his passionate love affairs with women like Hermione, there had been the fire of desire leaping between them. It had seemed to consume them both. Inevitably however, where he was concerned, it would soon die, without leaving even a glowing ember behind.

What he felt for Yseulta was quite different. From the moment she had looked up at him tremblingly on the train he had wanted to help and protect her. Every moment since then he had found himself thinking about her and being drawn towards her.

He had watched her in the kirk today. He knew that as she followed the service she was praying in a way he had always thought a woman should pray, not only with her lips, but with her soul.

If it had been Hermione, or any of his other loves standing beside him, they would have been acutely conscious of him. They would try by every means in their power to attract his attention. But Yseulta had been completely oblivious of him. He thought nothing could be more beautiful than when she had looked at the stained-glass window that had been erected by his grandfather. He had seen her profile against the darkness of the kirk walls.

'She is very lovely,' he told himself, 'and it is cruel that she should be treated by her uncle in such an appalling manner.'

Only to think of what she had suffered made him feel furious. He wanted, as he had done before, to put his arms around her and reassure her that she need never return to such purgatory.

He had been aware of her politeness and consideration for the older members of his party. And when she sat next to one of the elderly gentlemen at dinner he had noticed how she listened attentively to everything he had to say. At the same time, she made intelligent remarks.

The Duke knew that Hermione or any of the women like her would have been bored stiff at having to converse with anybody else except him. They would have done everything to draw his attention – touching him with their fingers, flirting with him in words and with the movements of their lips. They would have given him provocative little glances from under their eyelashes. It was all so familiar, something he expected as a matter of course.

He had in fact believed, where women were concerned, that everyone was the same. But Yseulta was different in every way. He found himself, when he looked at her, forgetting there were other members in the house party, and thinking only of her and her problems.

'I have to help her!' he told himself a thousand times but was not certain how he could do so.

When they had walked on the moors he had known, although he would not admit it to himself, that they were thinking the same thoughts. Although they did not talk, because she was with him, he had never felt so happy. Then when he had been threatened by one of his clan his first thoughts had been to protect Yseulta. Yet it was she who had protected him.

She had stood in front of him, and unexpectedly had solved the whole problem through her knowledge of Gaelic. Somehow it had not even seemed surprising that she should know a language that, apart from a few words, he did not know himself. She had calmed the demented man down, and together they had decided what was to be done for the family that was his responsibility.

'How could I marry anyone who would not feel like that about my people?' he asked himself,

He knew that Lady Beryl, who was very English, would be bored and fretful when they were in Scotland. Lady Deborah might laugh at his jokes, but she would have no idea what to do about a pregnant clanswoman in tears.

'Yseulta is mine!' he vowed to himself defiantly. 'I will marry her, whatever anyone says!'

He did not underestimate the difficulties that lay ahead, especially where his mother was concerned. She loved him, she was very proud of him, and like all mothers she would want the best for her son.

'How can I explain to her – how can I convince her that Yseulta *is* the best, where I am concerned?' he asked himself.

'If I cannot marry her,' he decided, 'I will go back and face the Earl, and if necessary, the divorce.'

But he knew that the last thing he wanted was to marry Hermione. Her beauty had attracted him, but if he was honest, he admitted they had nothing in common. He was quite certain that Hermione, without the crowds to admire her, would be utterly bored living at the castle.

The beauty of the moors, the river and the sea would not match the beauty she found in the reflection in her mirror.

"I will not lose Yseulta!" the Duke said aloud.

He knew then that he would fight for her, as he had never fought for anything in the whole of his life before.

CHAPTER SEVEN

The Duke was called early by his valet and rose to dress himself quickly. He had been dreaming of Yseulta and he was thinking of her as he walked along the passage towards the Breakfast Room. However Douglas was waiting for him on the landing.

"Good day, Yer Grace," he said, "I thought Yer Grace would wish to know that the wife of the clansman ye brought to the Castle yestereve had her baby early this morn'."

The Duke listened, then he said,

"I will go and see them."

He walked down the stairs and out through the front door towards the stables.

He saw the two little boys playing ball in the yard with one of the stable lads and went to the harness room. As he entered the small kitchen he was not surprised to see Yseulta standing at the window. The morning sun was on her hair, and he thought he might have known that she would be concerned with the new-born child.

He did not speak, but as if she sensed his presence she turned round and he saw that she held the baby in her arms. She looked across the small room at him and somehow the world stood still. Without either of them moving or speaking they were close to each other. For a moment the Duke felt as if they met across time and space and that nothing could divide them. Then Yseulta dropped her eyes and said a little shyly,

"Here is a new Clansman for Your Grace!"

The Duke walked towards her and as he did so the baby gave a tiny cry.

"I think," she said, "he wants his mother."

She carried the child from the room and the Duke could hear her talking next door. Then MacVegon came in from outside and he said to him,

"Congratulations! I hear you have another son. I hope your wife is all right."

The man muttered something in Gaelic, which the Duke knew were words of gratitude. Then once again he went down on one knee and kissed the Duke's hand.

The Duke went back to the castle and upstairs to the Breakfast Room. As he expected, the male members of his party were all hurrying to get to the river, and he realised that Lady Beryl and Lady Deborah were going with them. They had finished their breakfast, and the Duke took them downstairs and saw them into the brakes that were waiting for them.

"Are you not coming with us, Kenyon?" Hugo asked.

"I will join you later," the Duke replied. "I have some things to see to first."

"Then we will try to leave you a few salmon!" Anthony joked.

They waved as their brakes drove off, and the Duke watched them go. He had arranged the night before that the older members should fish at the lower part of the river. The younger men were to go to the top where the walking was rougher and the fishing more strenuous.

As he walked upstairs he thought that later Yseulta could come with him and how much he would enjoy teaching her to fish. He found his mother finishing her breakfast.

"Ah, there you are, Kenyon," she said. "I wondered what had happened to you."

"I have been seeing the new addition to the clan!" he replied.

The Duchess smiled.

"I hear that Mrs. MacVegon produced another son last night, and I have told Mrs. Ross to look out some shawls and clothes for him. Are you going fishing?"

"I want to see my factor first," the Duke said.

The Duchess knew without being told that her son was annoyed with the man.

"I think," she said gently, "that McKay is getting a little old for his job. I should suggest to him, Kenyon, that he retires. Then we can find a younger man to fill the post."

"I am sure that is the right thing to do, Mama," the Duke agreed.

As his mother was talking he had been helping himself to one of the hot dishes on the sideboard. Now as he sat down at the table the Duchess said,

"You have not forgotten the ball tomorrow night? I am hoping, Kenyon, that you will tell me..."

She was interrupted before she could say any more as Douglas came into the room and went to the Duke's side.

"The postman has just brought the letters, Yer Grace. I've put 'em in the study, but there's one marked, 'URGENT' for Miss Corde."

"Put it on the table," the Duke ordered. "She will be coming in for her breakfast shortly."

Douglas did as he was told and the Duchess rose to her feet.

"I have a lot to do, Kenyon," she said, "and I would like to speak to you alone later, when you have a few minutes to spare."

"Of course, Mama," the Duke replied.

He knew exactly what she wished to ask him and was wondering what she would say when he told her whom he had decided to marry. Then as Douglas reached the door, Yseulta came in. She had obviously run from the stables, knowing she was late for breakfast. Her cheeks were flushed and her hair was a little blown by the wind.

"I am sorry I am so late," she said apologetically, "but when I met the midwife who looked after Mrs. MacVegon she had a lot to tell me."

The Duke smiled.

"There is nothing the Scots enjoy more than a birth or a funeral!"

"Mama always told me that women are excluded from Scottish funerals," Yseulta replied, "but at least we have to be present at a birth!"

The Duke laughed then rose and walked to the sideboard.

"What would you like to eat?" he asked. "There is quite a large choice."

Yseulta stood beside him and thought it did not matter what she ate as long as she was with him. He helped her from a dish of small fish that were fresh from the sea. Then as he carried it to the table he said,

"There is a letter for you."

"A letter?" Yseulta exclaimed.

She looked at it, recognised the handwriting, and the Duke saw her go very pale.

"Eat your breakfast first," he advised.

"No … no," Yseulta replied. "This is from Uncle Lionel and I-I am sure he is very angry!"

The Duke was aware that her hands were trembling as she picked up the letter but thought it would be a mistake to argue with her. He sat down at his place at the top of the table watching her, as still standing, she opened the envelope. Very slowly she drew out the contents. The Duke clenched his fists as he saw how frightened she was and that not only her hands but her whole body was trembling. As if it was difficult to focus her eyes, she read slowly what was written and for a moment was very still. Then with a cry that was like that of an animal caught in a trap she flung the letter down on the table and ran from the room.

The Duke jumped to his feet and picking up the letter read what the Marquess had written.

'As you went to Scotland instead of returning here as you were told to do, I have instructed the Sheriff to send you back with a police escort. I intend to take the despicable Duke of Strathvegon to Court for the Abduction of a Minor. That will be his punishment, and you will receive yours when you return!

Derroncorde.'

The Duke stared at what was written as if he could hardly believe what he was reading. Then he knew that he must find Yseulta. He would tell her that he would not allow her to return to her uncle or be subjected to the punishment he intended to mete out to her.

He moved towards the door, then being so closely linked with Yseulta, his perception made him look out of the window. He saw her below him emerging through a side door and moving across the terrace down the steps into the garden. She was moving very quickly, and for a moment he wondered where she was going. Then he knew the answer.

Flinging the letter on the floor, he ran from the Breakfast Room down the stairs to the ground floor. He let himself out of the garden door by which Yseulta had emerged.

When he reached the terrace he had just a glimpse of her passing through the gate that led from the garden out on to the cliffs. Now he ran faster than he had ever run in his life before, knowing where she was going and what she intended to do.

At the end of the rough grass that bordered the land above the rocks and the beach there was a wooden jetty. It was built out into the bay to enable those who were going boating or sailing to step aboard without getting their feet wet.

By the time the Duke had reached the end of the rough land, Yseulta was at the end of the jetty looking down into the water beneath her. As the tide was in, the sea was deep at this point and at the same time it was rather rough. Yseulta was thinking that as she could not swim the waves would carry her away and it was only a question of seconds before she would be drowned.

'Please help me, Papa,' she prayed.

Then the Duke's arms were round her, pulling her back from the edge of the jetty, and holding her tightly against him. For a moment it was difficult to realise he was there. Then she cried out,

"No, *no* – do not stop me. There is nothing else I can do!"

"How can you want to do anything so wrong – *so wicked* – as to try to drown yourself?" the Duke asked.

His voice was very deep. At the same time, because he had run so fast his breath was coming fitfully.'

"I-I *have to!*" Yseulta cried. "Do you not understand? Uncle Lionel is planning to cause a scandal that will hurt you but ... if I am dead you will be safe."

"You are thinking of *me!*" the Duke said wonderingly. "My sweet, my precious darling, how can you be so ridiculous? If I lost you I would lose the only thing that ever mattered to me in the whole world!"

Yseulta looked up at him.

"B-but you must not want me!" she stammered. "I can only harm you!"

"The only thing that could really harm me," the Duke replied, "Is if I should lose you."

He pulled her even closer to him as he spoke and because it was impossible to resist him, she hid her face against his shoulder.

"You are mine," he said, "*mine!* If we have to fight the whole world to be together, that is what we will do!"

Because he spoke so determinedly, Yseulta felt as if she must cry at his kindness. Instead she looked up at him to say,

"Please listen to me, you must not save me! I love you. I love you with all my heart, but because I love you I cannot allow you to be hurt, or slandered or laughed at!"

The Duke looked down at her and his eyes were very tender as he said,

"That is how I want my wife to think of me, to protect me and to love me."

He saw that Yseulta was going to protest again, and he said,

"We are going back, my precious love, to 'Face the music', and whatever anyone may say, we are not going to lose each other."

"It is wrong for you," Yseulta whispered.

"It is right for me!" the Duke contradicted. "Completely and absolutely right because you are mine, and I need you."

With his arm round her waist he drew her back along the jetty and across the rough ground until they reached the gate into the garden. It was then, sheltered by a tree and hidden from the castle by the wall that ran down to the bottom of the garden, that the Duke put both his arms around her.

"I love you," he said, "and nothing in the world matters beside our love."

Yseulta parted her lips to answer him, but his mouth was on hers. He kissed her until it was impossible to think of anything but the beating of her heart and the sensations he aroused in her. He made her feel once again as if she was flying to the stars. Only when they both felt as if they had entered Paradise did they come back to earth. As the Duke opened the gate into the garden and they went inside, Yseulta said in a frightened little voice,

"What shall I do when the Sheriff takes me away?"

"I have the answer to that," the Duke said, "and we will go into my study and talk about it."

She looked at him a little uncertainly, and he took her hand in his as they walked across the lawn and up the steps on to the terrace. They were just about to enter the castle by the same door through which they had left it when Douglas appeared.

"The Sheriff's here ter see Yer Grace," he announced, "and he's brought a policeman wi' him. He's waiting outside in the carriage!"

Yseulta gave a stifled little cry, and as the Duke knew she wanted to run away his fingers tightened on her hand.

"Where is the Sheriff waiting for me, Douglas?" he asked.

"In the study, Yer Grace, and he says he wishes ter speak to Yer Grace on business."

"Ask Her Grace to join us in the study," the Duke ordered, "and I will be there in a few minutes."

"Verra good, Yer Grace," Douglas replied and walked away.

Yseulta looked up at the Duke frantically.

"I could run away and h-hide," she said, "and perhaps when he is gone, I can go where no one will find me then, if you could give me a little money, I will disappear."

The Duke smiled.

"I think, my darling," he said, "that wherever you go everyone will be very curious about you, because you are so lovely."

"B-but the Sheriff is taking me away," Yseulta said as if she felt he did not understand, "and the Police will force me to go back to my Uncle Lionel!"

The Duke drew her into the house. Holding her tightly by the hand so she could not escape he took her into a small writing room that was on the Ground Floor and seldom used.

He shut the door. Then he said,

"Listen to me, my precious. I want you to trust me."

"You know I do," Yseulta answered, "but you must understand that Uncle Lionel is a very vindictive man. He is determined to ruin you in every way he can!"

She gave a little sob and went on,

"If he says he is going to bring a case against you, then that is what he will do and he will make sure that everybody talks about you and it is reported in the newspapers."

"I know exactly what he intends," the Duke replied, "but I have the answer."

"You have?" Yseulta asked.

There was just a touch of hope in her voice and in her eyes. The Duke released her hand and put his arms around her.

"I love you, and I know you love me," he said. "Will you promise me to do exactly what I tell you?"

"I will do anything ... anything you want," Yseulta said, "but..."

"There are no 'buts' the Duke said. "Just swear to me on everything you hold sacred that you will do what I tell you."

There was a solemn note in his voice and after a second Yseulta said,

"I promise."

The Duke pulled her closer, and his lips found hers. He kissed her demandingly, possessively, until she felt as if he drew not only her heart but also her soul from her body and made them his.

Then he released her and said,

"Now let us go and send the Sheriff away, so that we can talk about ourselves."

He did not wait for her to answer but opened the door. Taking her again by the hand, he led her up the stairs and along the passage to his study. As they reached it, they saw Douglas waiting to open the door for them. The Duke felt the tremor of fear that went through Yseulta.

He knew then that he would dedicate his whole life to preventing her from ever being so afraid as she was at this moment. Douglas opened the door and they walked in.

The Duchess was sitting in an armchair beside the fireplace. The Sheriff, who was a tall, upstanding man of about fifty, was standing beside her. As the Duke entered the room he walked towards him, holding out his hand.

"Good morning, Your Grace, it is delightful to see you again, and I am only sorry that the reason for my visit is an unpleasant one."

"The Sheriff tells me," the Duchess interposed, "that the Marquess of Derroncorde is insisting that his niece Yseulta is returned to him immediately, and he intends, although it seems incredible, to take action against you in an English Court!"

"So I have already learned," the Duke replied. "But unfortunately for the Marquess, it is something he will be unable to do."

"I am afraid," the Sheriff said somewhat deprecatingly, "that the Marquess of Derroncorde, as Miss Yseulta Corde's guardian, is within his rights."

"He has instructed you, I understand," the Duke said quietly, "to arrange for the return of his niece, Miss Yseulta Corde."

"That is correct," the Sheriff agreed.

"But it is impossible!"

"Impossible?" the Sheriff repeated looking puzzled.

"Completely impossible," the Duke affirmed, "for the simple reason that Miss Yseulta Corde no longer exists!"

The Duchess looked surprised, and the Sheriff stared at the Duke in astonishment while Yseulta gave a little gasp. Then the Duke slipping her arm through his covered it with his hand.

"May I, Sheriff," he asked in a different tone of voice, "introduce you to my wife, the Duchess of Strathvegon!"

There was absolute silence for a moment. Then the Duke turned to look at Yseulta's wide and frightened eyes and said gently,

"Tell the Sheriff, my darling, that you are my wife. "

He pressed her hand with his fingers as he spoke, and as if she was a puppet and he was pulling the strings she said in a very low voice,

"I am your ... wife!"

As if the Sheriff understood what had happened, his eyes were twinkling as he held out his hand.

"Let me congratulate Your Grace," he said. "Of course, I now understand that in the circumstances my journey here has been quite unnecessary."

"Not entirely," the Duke said, "for I want you to register the fact that we are married, and also that you and my mother were our witnesses."

It was then that the Duchess found her voice.

"How could I have dreamt," she asked, "how could I have imagined that you, Kenyon, would have a 'Marriage by Consent'?"

Then she gave a little exclamation.

"This is something no one else must know about except ourselves!"

"That is what I thought, too," the Duke said, "and tomorrow night at the ball, as you intended, you shall announce my engagement. It can be put in *The*

Gazette' before the Marquess hears from our friend the Sheriff that he no longer has any jurisdiction over his niece."

He turned to the Sheriff and said,

"I am sure we can trust you to keep our secret and allow my mother to announce our engagement, which will be followed by our wedding – which can be attended by all the clan."

"Your Grace can trust me to carry out your wishes," the Sheriff said, "but of course there is one condition – that I am invited to your wedding!"

"You shall be Guest of Honour!" the Duke smiled. "And now, I think you should be the first to drink a toast to my bride and to our happiness."

"Nothing could give me greater pleasure!" the Sheriff replied.

When the Duke a little later escorted him to the front door, the Duchess was left alone with Yseulta. For a moment the two women just looked at each other, then Yseulta went down on her knees beside the Duchess's chair.

"Forgive me, forgive me!" she begged. "I know it is wrong to marry your son when he is so important but when I tried to save him by drowning myself, he stopped me!"

The Duchess gave a little cry of horror.

"Is that why you were running through the garden? But, my dear child, how could you wish to do anything so wrong?"

"I wanted to save him from the wicked things Uncle Lionel would say about him, but I am afraid he will still say them."

"Then we must do everything in our power to prevent it," the Duchess replied.

"But how ... how can we do that?" Yseulta cried helplessly.

There were tears in her eyes as she looked up at the older woman and said,

"I love him. I love him with all my heart! I would rather have died than have him derided in any way."

The Duchess put out her hand and laid it on her shoulder.

"My dear," she said, "you are exactly the wife I wanted Kenyon to find – someone who would love him for himself and not because he is a Duke."

She sighed before she went on,

"But since we are all clever people, I cannot believe that we will find a way of preventing him from being hurt."

"Please try to do that," Yseulta pleaded. "I will do anything, anything you tell me to do."

The Duchess was still for a moment. Then she said,

"Was I dreaming, or did someone say that your mother was a Sinclair?"

"Yes, Mama was a Sinclair, and that is why I have always longed to come to Scotland. When she was young she lived in Caithness."

"That certainly makes things easier," the Duchess said as if she was speaking to herself.

But before she could explain why, the door opened and the Duke returned.

"I am sorry, Mama, if this had been a shock to you," he said, walking towards his mother. "I was going to tell you how much I love Yseulta, but this morning she received a letter from her uncle telling her of his diabolical plan to humiliate her – and me!"

"He is behaving in the most appalling manner!" the Duchess said. "Now I have a lot to think about and plan for tomorrow night, so I am going to leave you two together, which is what I am sure you want."

"You are being marvellous, Mama, as I knew you would be," the Duke said.

"When we announce your engagement," the Duchess said, "we shall take the first obstacle in our stride, then I have to think about the next one."

She smiled at her son, then turned towards Yseulta and kissed her cheek.

"I am delighted to have a Scottish daughter-in-law," she said softly.

She went from the room and as the door shut behind her Yseulta flung herself against the Duke.

"How can you have been so clever, so wonderful, as to marry me in that strange manner?" she asked. "You have saved me from having to go back to Uncle Lionel!"

"Now you are my wife nothing and nobody shall ever hurt you again!" the Duke vowed.

"Is it really, completely legal?" Yseulta asked hesitatingly.

"As a Scot, you should know that it is the law of Scotland that if two people declare before witnesses that they are man and wife, they are as legally married as if they were in a cathedral or a kirk."

Yseulta drew in a deep breath as if a burden had been lifted from her shoulders.

"I can hardly believe it!" she cried. "It is the most wonderful, the most glorious thing that has ever happened to me!"

The Duke drew her close.

"That is what I want you to think," he said, "and go on thinking for the rest of our lives."

Then he was kissing her and it was impossible to think of anything but the magic and wonder of their love.

*

When they joined the others at the river later in the day, the Duke taught Yseulta how to fish and she caught her first salmon. She was so thrilled and delighted that the others teased her. They said she would have to have it mounted or else no one would ever believe that she had caught it all by herself.

As soon as they got back to the castle, Anthony insisted that the girls practised the reels, which he had arranged with the Duchess to take place the next night. The Duke joined in and he realised how gracefully Yseulta danced. It was impossible for him to watch anything but the happiness in her eyes and the smile on her lips. Then when the men went to dress for dinner Hugo said to the Duke,

"I want to speak to you a moment."

They went into the study, and to his surprise his friend, whom he had known ever since they had been at school together, looked somewhat embarrassed.

"What is it, Hugo?" the Duke asked.

It seemed for a moment as if Hugo could not find the words to say what was in his mind. Then he said,

"I have, of course, an idea as to why your mother decided to give a ball at this particular moment, and why the girls were asked to come to Scotland to meet you."

"I expect you also guessed that George Wallington was threatening to kill me!" the Duke said.

"Knowing Wallington, we were all afraid that is what would happen," Hugo replied.

There was silence, then after a moment he went on,

"I just wondered whether you had made up your mind which of the three girls you are going to ask to be your wife."

The Duke raised his eyebrows before he asked,

"Does it particularly matter to you?"

"As a matter of fact, it does!" Hugo answered. "You know as well as I do, Kenyon, that neither Deborah nor Beryl would be allowed to refuse a Duke."

"And you are interested in Deborah," the Duke remarked.

Hugo walked across the study floor and back again.

"I am not a Duke," he said, "but when my father dies I shall be a peer, my mother is American and, as you know, I am extremely rich. If you are not in the running, I am quite certain that Fernhurst would welcome me with open arms."

The Duke laughed.

"My dear Hugo, you have my warmest congratulations!"

"Do you mean that?" Hugo asked eagerly.

"Considering all the years we have been together, I think you would know if I was lying to you," the Duke replied.

He thought as he spoke that he had never seen his friend look so happy.

"You will hardly believe it, Kenyon," he said, "but this time I am really in love, which is something I never thought would happen – but it has!"

"I am delighted!" the Duke said. "You must tell me what you want as a wedding present."

"It will have to be something really expensive," Hugo joked.

Saying they would be late for dinner if they did not hurry, the Duke managed to escape without his friend asking point-blank if he intended to marry Lady Beryl. As he dressed for dinner, he thought with a faint twist of his lips that the one person who would be very relieved by the announcement of his engagement would be Lady Beryl Wood. He had learned from his mother that she was very much in love with somebody else.

He thought that only Fate, or perhaps the Good Fairy who had attended his christening, could have managed to make him avoid the pitfall of marrying a girl who only wanted his title. Instead he had been given one who filled his heart as he filled hers.

*

If the Duke was happy, to Yseulta it was as if her whole world was filled with a dazzling light.

'I love him! *I love him!'* she said as she bathed before dinner.

"I love him!" she said as her maid helped her into a beautiful gown that the seamstresses had altered for her.

"I love him!" her feet seemed to tap out as she ran down the passage because she was so eager to see him again. He was waiting for her in the drawing room, looking resplendent in his evening clothes, a jabot at his neck. There were other people there, but as their eyes looked into each other's they said privately in their hearts,

"I love you! *I love you!'*

Dinner seemed to be more delicious and more impressive than it had been before. The piper played his pipes round the table and Yseulta felt as if every note was a paean of happiness within her. This was her land as well as the Duke's and she was a part of it. Now she could live in its beauty and its glory as she had always wanted to do. Then after they had sat talking in the drawing room, the Duchess rose to her feet to say,

"As we are all going to be very late tomorrow night, I am going to send you to bed early."

The men protested laughingly, but the Duchess was adamant.

The girls bade her goodnight, while her older friends who had spent a long day at the river were only too willing to retire. Finally when everybody, with the exception of the Duke and Yseulta, had left the drawing room she said,

"I have something to tell you, and I hope you will think it good news."

Yseulta looked at her a little apprehensively.

The Duke, as if he was afraid it might be something that would upset Yseulta, put his arm round her shoulders.

"What is it, Mama?" he asked.

"I have been in touch, this afternoon," the Duchess replied, "with Sir John Sinclair who, as you know, Kenyon, is the 6th Baronet and chieftain of the Sinclairs in Caithness-shire."

The Duke was listening intently as his mother went on,

"Sir John lives at Dunbeath Castle, which is only a short distance from here, and I visited him this afternoon."

The Duchess looked at Yseulta as she said,

"He is delighted to hear that his cousin is to marry my son, and tomorrow night he will announce your engagement at the ball."

"He does not mind doing that?" Yseulta asked in a low voice.

"He was honoured to be asked," the Duchess assured her, "and he knows nothing, I repeat, nothing about your father. Nor, I think, does anybody else in this part of Scotland."

Yseulta reached out to take hold of the Duke's hand, and his fingers tightened on hers.

"What the Scottish will learn," the Duchess said slowly, "Is that your grandfather was the 5th Baronet who died in 1842, and he was a direct descendent, as all the Sinclairs are, of the Earls of Caithness."

The Duchess paused before she went on,

"No one could be more respected and admired than Sir John, and he will, on announcing your engagement, say that you are the granddaughter of the 5th Baronet, and that your paternal grandfather was the 2nd Marquess of Derroncorde She smiled at Yseulta and after a moment continued,

"There was no need even to mention your uncle in the report of the engagement, which I have already sent to the newspapers."

Yseulta looked up at the Duke, tears in her eyes.

"That was very astute of you, Mama," the Duke said. "I might have known that you would overcome the last obstacle in style!"

The Duchess laughed.

"There is still one more before your wedding," she said, "which will take place next Saturday. We have to provide your bride with a trousseau."

She smiled at Yseulta and went on,

"So I have arranged for a number of the latest and most exciting gowns available to be brought from Inverness by your train which left this afternoon to fetch them."

The Duke gave a shout of delight and kissed his mother.

"Mama, you are a genius!"

"No, she is the Fairy Godmother we needed to complete our fairy story!" Yseulta murmured.

Tears were running down her cheeks, but they were tears of happiness, and as the Duchess left the room the Duke wiped them away.

"If you cry," he said, "I shall believe that you are already becoming tired of me!"

"How can you say anything so ridiculous?" Yseulta laughed. "How could I ever, ever be tired of anyone so wonderful as you?"

"That is what you have to go on thinking," the Duke said, "for the next sixty years, at least!"

He kissed her, then they walked along the passage, linked together, to Yseulta's bedroom. As they entered they saw a small fire burning in the grate because it was cold in the evening. There were three candles in the candle-holder by the curtained bed. He looked at her for a long moment before he said,

"You realise, my precious, that you are my wife, but if you want me to wait until after our wedding in the kirk, I will do so."

Yseulta put her arms around his neck.

"I am ... yours," she whispered, "completely and absolutely. All I want is for you to love me."

"That is what I wanted you to say," he answered.

He kissed her gently and went from the room. Yseulta undressed, and then before she got into bed she pulled back the curtains. The stars were shining over the sea and the moonlight glittered on the waves.

She knew that if she had done as she intended, she would no longer be alive. Instead, she was starting a new life. A life that she knew would be filled with love and a happiness she had not known since her mother had died.

'Thank You, God,' she said fervently. '*Thank You, thank You.*'

She thought that among the stars she could see her father smiling at her and telling her that against all odds she had won a difficult race. As Yseulta left the window and got into bed her heart was beating frantically as she waited. Then as the flames of the fire seemed to leap up to illuminate the room, the Duke came in. For a moment she felt shy. Then as he came slowly towards her she put out her hands.

He took them in his and sat down facing her.

"You are perfect, my darling!" he said. "I would not do anything that you feel is wrong, or if you would rather have time to think about our marriage before I make you my wife."

"I-I do not have to think," Yseulta replied, "but only to feel how incredibly wonderful you are and that love – however it comes, is a gift from God and how can I possibly refuse it?"

The Duke smiled.

"Only you could think of the right answer," he said, "and that, my precious little wife, is what I think about you."

He got into bed beside her, and pulled her close to him, but for a moment he did not kiss her. He only lay looking at her, the firelight glittering on her hair. He could see her large eyes looking up at him and now they were no longer afraid.

Instead they were filled with a love that was very different, he thought, from the way any other woman had looked at him. He knew that Yseulta, as she had already proved, wanted to protect him from anything that might hurt him.

Her love was utterly selfless, so that she had no thought for herself, but only for him. He had also known when he had seen her this morning, holding the new-born baby in her arms, that she would love their children.

Whether they lived in a castle or a Pictish fort, as long as they were together it would be home – a home that was part of their hearts. Because he was silent, Yseulta looked at him enquiringly.

"Suppose," she said in a very small voice, "now that we are married, you are disappointed in me?"

The Duke laughed, and it was a very happy sound.

"Do you think that possible?" he asked. "I was just thinking how perfect you were, and that everything about you is so angelic, so different from any other woman, that I am the most fortunate man in the whole world!"

Yseulta gave a little cry of joy.

"Oh, darling," she said, "please teach me to love you as you want to be loved. Save me from making mistakes and I will try to be everything that you have ever wanted in a wife."

"You *are* everything I have ever wanted!" the Duke said, and his voice was deep.

Then he was kissing her – kissing her until the room was filled with stars that glittered not only in her eyes, but in her breast, and in their hearts. As the moon shone on the sea and on the quietness of the moors, Yseulta felt as if the whole beauty and glory of Scotland was in his kisses.

"I love you... *I love you!*" she whispered.

The Duke said the same words a thousand times during the night.

It was a tune played on the pipes, carried on the wind, and their hearts were in the Highlands for all eternity.

Printed in Dunstable, United Kingdom

81660817R00109